Fargo aimed carefully over Sarah's shoulder at Logan's head and said, "Let go of Miss Gallagher." Logan didn't move.

Fargo pulled back the hammer of the .45.

"You can't shoot," Logan said. "You might hit Miss Gallagher."

The way he said *Miss* made it sound like something nasty, and Fargo was tempted to shoot him just for that. He might have done it, too, if Slater hadn't thrown a rock and hit him on the shoulder.

When the rock hit Fargo, Logan shoved Sarah at him as hard as he could. She stumbled into Fargo, throwing him farther off balance. Before he could recover, Slater grabbed his wrist and twisted. Logan threw Sarah to the ground, then slugged Fargo in the stomach with a hard right fist. Before he could hit him again, Fargo did the only thing he could think of. He kicked the soldier right in the crotch, and Logan sank to the ground clutching himself, moaning, and drooling. . . .

THE TRAILSMAN
#287

CALIFORNIA CAMEL CORPS

by

Jon Sharpe

A SIGNET BOOK

SIGNET
Published by New American Library, a division of
Penguin Group (USA) Inc., 375 Hudson Street,
New York, New York 10014, USA
Penguin Group (Canada), 90 Eglinton Avenue East, Suite 700, Toronto,
Ontario M4P 2Y3, Canada (a division of Pearson Penguin Canada Inc.)
Penguin Books Ltd., 80 Strand, London WC2R 0RL, England
Penguin Ireland, 25 St. Stephen's Green, Dublin 2,
Ireland (a division of Penguin Books Ltd.)
Penguin Group (Australia), 250 Camberwell Road, Camberwell, Victoria 3124,
Australia (a division of Pearson Australia Group Pty. Ltd.)
Penguin Books India Pvt. Ltd., 11 Community Centre, Panchsheel Park,
New Delhi - 110 017, India
Penguin Group (NZ), cnr Airborne and Rosedale Roads, Albany,
Auckland 1310, New Zealand (a division of Pearson New Zealand Ltd.)
Penguin Books (South Africa) (Pty.) Ltd., 24 Sturdee Avenue,
Rosebank, Johannesburg 2196, South Africa

Penguin Books Ltd., Registered Offices:
80 Strand, London WC2R 0RL, England

First published by Signet, an imprint of New American Library,
a division of Penguin Group (USA) Inc.

First Printing, September 2005
10 9 8 7 6 5 4 3 2 1

The first chapter of this book previously appeared in *Texas Terror Trail*, the
two hundred eighty-sixth volume in this series.

Copyright © Penguin Group (USA) Inc., 2005
All rights reserved

 REGISTERED TRADEMARK—MARCA REGISTRADA

Printed in the United States of America

The Trailsman

Beginnings . . . they bend the tree and they mark the man. Skye Fargo was born when he was eighteen. Terror was his midwife, vengeance his first cry. Killing spawned Skye Fargo, ruthless, cold-blooded murder. Out of the acrid smoke of gunpowder still hanging in the air, he rose, cried out a promise never forgotten.

The Trailsman they began to call him all across the West: searcher, scout, hunter, the man who could see where others only looked, his skills for hire but not his soul, the man who lived each day to the fullest, yet trailed each tomorrow. Skye Fargo, the Trailsman, the seeker who could take the wildness of a land and the wanting of a woman and make them his own.

Fort Defiance, Arizona, 1857—Skye Fargo has been hired to help lead a camel caravan to California for the U.S. Army. The camels are bad enough. The Navajo and the killers are much worse.

1

Skye Fargo watched as the four horses ran full-out toward the distant finish line. One of the Indian ponies had fallen back, but the other, a pinto ridden by Short Knife, was moving up. It was about to pass the little roan ridden by a trooper named Logan, and when it did, it would certainly overtake the leader, a bay with Corporal Slater in the stripped-down saddle.

Fargo took in the scene, the flying hooves of the straining horses kicking up clods of dirt, distorted a little in his view by the heat waves rising from the ground; the riders leaning forward, low over the necks of their mounts almost as if whispering some secret instructions in their ears; the crowd of men waving their arms, yelling, and jumping around to urge their favorite on.

It was a scene that had been repeated for many years. Before the Americans had come into this part of the country and founded Fort Defiance, the Indians and Spanish had met at a spot that was surprisingly green thanks to its flowing springs. There they traded horses, raced them, and gambled on the outcome. After the arrival of the Americans, the tradition had continued, though somewhat uneasily, as the Navajo trusted the Americans even less than they trusted the Spanish.

And Fargo thought that they might have had good reason. His lake-blue eyes narrowed as he saw that Logan had edged his horse dangerously close to the pinto.

Short Knife's attention was concentrated only on the horse in front of him. He had no idea that Logan was so close, and getting even closer.

1

Fargo wasn't the only one who saw what was happening, however. The cheering that had been coming from the Navajos changed abruptly into shouts of warning, and the yells of the soldiers dropped in volume as they craned their necks to see if the apparent collision would actually occur.

It did. The roan bumped the pinto, but instead of merely nudging the pony off stride, the roan somehow managed to trip it, causing its legs to tangle. The pinto went down in a dust cloud, throwing Short Knife forward.

The Navajo somersaulted once, then rolled and lay still as the roan thundered past, its hooves barely missing his head.

While nearly everyone else ran to see if Short Knife was dead and if the pinto had broken a leg in its fall, Fargo remained where he was, watching the end of the race.

Not that there was any doubt who would win, not now. Slater's horse increased its lead over the other two, and in fact Logan seemed to have no interest in winning. Fargo wondered if he had bet on Slater.

"He can always claim it was an accident," said a gravelly voice behind Fargo.

Fargo turned around to see who'd spoken. It was Carter, a career sergeant who looked as if he'd been in the desert far too long. His face was burned dark brown where it wasn't covered by a bristly gray beard, and his skin was crosshatched with wrinkles. He had developed a permanent squint that made him look as if he was always peering off into the distance. He was a head shorter than Fargo, and skinny as a rake.

"Might get away with callin' it an accident, too," Carter said. "Be hard for anybody to prove any different."

"But you don't believe it was an accident," Fargo said.

"Hell, no. Not any more than you do." Carter pointed a skinny finger. "See there? Slater's crossed over the line. There'll be some boys won money or silver on his ride, and they'll side with Logan, no matter what he says."

"What about the Indians?"

"Hell, what can they do? They ain't about to start

2

anything here. They're outnumbered and outgunned. Kin' hozhoni, now, he might be a different story."

Kin' hozhoni was better known as Manuelito, one of the Navajo chiefs, a man who'd given the army a certain amount of trouble in the past and figured to continue to do so.

"Manuelito's not here, though," Fargo pointed out.

"No," Carter said. "He's not." The sergeant spit into the dirt at his feet and wiped his mouth with the back of his hand. "But it just so happens that Short Knife's his cousin. What do you think about that?"

"I think we'd better go see if Short Knife's all right," Fargo said, and the two of them started in the direction of the fallen man.

By the time they got to him, the other Navajo men had surrounded Short Knife. They were muttering words that Fargo couldn't quite make out, but he knew they weren't friendly expressions of peace and brotherhood. Fargo and Carter wouldn't have been able to break into their circle even if they'd wanted to, which they didn't.

"They're tryin' to calm him down," Carter said. "Even if he's hurt, he'll be mighty mad about what happened. But, like I said, they don't want a fight."

"Do you?" Fargo asked.

"You must be jokin', Fargo."

They walked past the ring of men over to where Logan stood beside his winded horse. Several other troopers stood nearby, but most of them had gone farther on down to the finish line where they were congratulating Slater on his victory.

"Did you see what that son of a bitch did?" Logan said to anyone who would listen. "Tried to bump me out of the race. Serves him right that his horse stumbled and fell."

Fargo looked at Carter, who shrugged. "I told you he might could get away with callin' it an accident, but I never thought he had the brass to blame it on the Indian."

"You think anybody believes him?"

"Hell, no. But ain't nobody gonna call him on it." Carter cut his eyes at Fargo. " 'Less you do."

Fargo didn't want to get involved in an argument that

3

wasn't really any of his business. He was at Fort Defiance as a civilian employee, and he wasn't there to settle disputes between the fort and the Indians. He'd been hired to do the kind of job he did best, which was to lead a party from here to there through the toughest terrain and help everyone arrive safely at the end of the trail. Because of his ability in that kind of job, he'd earned the nickname of the Trailsman, and his work had led him to Fort Defiance to help lead an expedition. But he had to admit that it was the strangest job he'd ever taken on.

"We oughta check out the Indian's horse," Carter said.

Fargo walked over to where the animal stood. It hobbled away at his approach, but he could tell that it wasn't seriously hurt. The Navajos had probably already decided that. They weren't likely to neglect a good horse, even when a man was injured.

"The horse will be all right," Fargo said.

Carter looked the animal over and nodded. "I believe you're right." Then he glanced up and said, "Well, there comes Slater. He looks plumb satisfied with the whole thing, just like he didn't know what happened behind him."

It was possible that Slater really didn't know what had happened, Fargo thought. He'd been in front of the other two horses, and he couldn't have seen what was going on. On the other hand, it was also possible that Slater and Logan had worked something out between them before the race.

Even if they had, Fargo told himself, it was still none of his business. He heard shouting behind him and turned to see what was happening.

Short Knife had broken through the ring of men who surrounded him and was running toward Logan. He was holding a knife, and his face was twisted with hate.

"Goddamn it," Carter said.

"I thought you said the Indians didn't want a fight."

"*They* don't, but it sure as to God looks like Short Knife does. We gotta stop him."

Fargo thought that *we* was the wrong word, and he wasn't even sure who Carter intended to stop, since Logan seemed well aware of what Short Knife was up to. He even seemed to welcome it, having broken into

4

a big grin when he saw the Indian charging in his direction. Fargo's first instinct was to stay out of it, but when Carter broke into a short-legged trot, Fargo followed him. And then overtook him. Fargo's legs were a lot longer than Carter's, and the Trailsman was more accustomed to exercise that didn't involve riding a horse.

Fargo hadn't gotten far when he realized why Logan was grinning. He hadn't been carrying a weapon when he'd ridden in the race, of course, but at some time since he'd dismounted, someone had given him a pistol. He was holding it casually now, but Fargo could tell he was just waiting for Short Knife to get a little closer.

Short Knife either didn't see the pistol or didn't care. His friends were running after him in an attempt to head him off, but Fargo could see that they weren't going to be able to get to him in time.

So Fargo figured it was up to him.

He was closer to Logan than anyone, and he approached him from the right side. When he was about ten yards away, he called out, "Logan!"

The trooper, surprised, turned to see who was yelling. Fargo's long strides had propelled the Trailsman across the ground between them by that time. He grabbed Logan's wrist with both hands, twisted hard, and pulled down. The pistol fell to the ground.

Logan was infuriated. He hit Fargo on the side of the head with his left fist. Fargo was stunned, but he hadn't let go of his wrist. He shook his head to clear it, then whirled around, swinging Logan like a bag of meal before letting him go.

Logan tried to keep his feet, but he couldn't quite manage it. He danced across the ground for a few yards and fell on his stomach before skidding to a stop. He pushed himself up and started to jump to his feet, but Carter said, "Stay right there, Trooper."

Logan looked around to see who'd called out, and when he saw Carter, his face reddened. But he stayed where he was.

Short Knife had reached Fargo by that time. "You should not have done that."

"He was going to shoot you," Fargo said. "I didn't think that was a good idea."

5

"He cheated me. He caused my horse to fall. He could have killed me. And the horse. It is a matter of honor that we should fight."

"I'm sorry I got in the way," Fargo said. "But he had a pistol, and you didn't. I don't like the idea of people getting killed, even when it's a matter of honor."

Short Knife was tall, with shoulders almost as broad as Fargo's own. He had dark, angry eyes under heavy, ridged brows, and his black hair was held in place by a braided leather band that went around his head. He shoved his knife back into its leather scabbard and said, "Then you do not understand honor."

"Maybe not," Fargo agreed. "But I understand killing, and I don't like it. It usually just brings more trouble and killing along with it. You don't seem to be hurt too bad, and your horse is going to be fine. Why don't you forget this ever happened and go on home."

Short Knife looked at him with contempt. "I will never forget. I have been cheated." He looked around at the other Navajos who had now joined him. "My friends have been cheated."

"Nobody's been cheated," Carter said. "There won't be any payoff on the race. I'm disqualifyin' everybody."

"You can't do that!"

Slater had reached the group by that time. He was a small man, not much bigger than Carter, just the right size to be riding in a horse race where a couple of pounds in a man's weight made a big difference. He didn't like the idea of disqualification at all.

"I won the race fair and square," he said. "You can ask anybody."

He didn't mean that, Fargo knew. He meant, "You can ask any of my friends."

"I don't see what the problem is," Slater continued. "I crossed the line first. That's all that matters."

Carter turned to look at him. "Maybe that's because you didn't see what happened."

"No," Slater said. "I didn't, but it doesn't matter. Like I said, I crossed the finish line before anybody else. That makes me the winner."

"No, it just makes you the one who crossed the line. There was an accident, and Short Knife's pony fell."

6

"It wasn't an accident," Logan said. "He tried to bump my horse, and his own mount wound up falling. It was his own fault that he lost. You can't blame Slater for it."

If two of Short Knife's friends hadn't reached out and taken hold of his arms, he would have jumped on Logan then. As it was, he strained against the hands that held him. The cords in his neck stood out, and a vein throbbed in his forehead.

"Nobody's at fault," Carter said, not looking at Fargo. "We're just gonna call this whole thing off and forget about it. Short Knife's gonna go home, and in a few weeks we'll have another race. And nobody's horse better fall down."

"I won't be here in a few weeks," Slater said. "I'll be headed to California."

"So will I," Logan said.

"Yeah," Carter said. "I know. That's just too damn bad, ain't it. Now break this up and let's forget about it."

One look at Short Knife's face was all Fargo needed to know that the Indian wasn't going to forget anything. And the Trailsman didn't think Logan or Slater would, either.

"It's a long way to California," he said to Carter a few minutes later, after the soldiers and Indians had finally gone their separate ways. "I wish Logan and Slater were staying here."

"I think it's better that they're goin'. That way we won't be riskin' another Indian war every time there's a horse race."

"I don't think there'll be any more races for a while, not the way Short Knife's feeling. They won't be coming back here."

"I can't help that, and maybe it's a good thing, anyway. You and I won't be around to worry about it. We'll be heading off to California—with those damn camels."

Fargo had tried not to think of the camels. He was regretting that he'd taken the job of leading the expedition to California.

"I wonder how a camel would do in a race with a horse," he said. "You ever ride one?"

"Hell, no," Carter said. "I hate those sons of bitches."

7

2

The way Fargo saw it, it was all Jefferson Davis's fault even if he hadn't been the one to start it. Not the fact that Fargo was at Fort Defiance. He couldn't blame Davis for that.

But he could blame him for the camels.

If you wanted to go all the way back to the beginning, though, you'd have to blame the folks who signed the treaty at Guadalupe Hidalgo in 1848, ending almost two years of war between the United States and Mexico.

By the terms of the treaty, Mexico gave up over a million acres of land to the States, including the area around Fort Defiance. Much of the land was desert and rugged mountain ranges. There weren't any roads, and there weren't any navigable rivers, so exploration of all that new property was going to be quite a challenge. And one of the explorers, an army lieutenant named Crosman, came up with the idea of using camels to help do the job.

His idea was that camels, which after all had a lot more strength and endurance than horses, not to mention an ability to function for far longer without water, would be perfect for traveling the wide-open and arid spaces of the Southwest. Their big two-toed feet were perfect for desert travel, and they didn't even have to be shod. Crosman worked up what must have been a fairly convincing argument and managed to persuade a higher-ranking officer, Major Henry Wayne, that the idea had merit. Wayne was the one who took the idea to Jefferson Davis, who was a U.S. senator from Mississippi at the time.

Like Wayne before him, Davis liked what he heard about the camels. After all, he wasn't going to be the one who had to ride them or train them. So when he was appointed secretary of war in 1853, he started pushing Wayne's ideas to the Congress and the president. Both parties were skeptical of the plan to use camels in place of horses and mules, which had always proved reliable enough in the past, but Davis didn't give up. Eventually he managed to convince Congress to make an appropriation for the purchase of a small number of camels so the army could test whether they could be adapted to the American countryside.

Thirty or so camels were bought and shipped to Indianola, in south Texas, where Major Wayne took charge of them. It didn't take the camels long to prove that they had the advantage over both horses and mules when it came to hauling a load. A single camel could carry four times as much hay as a mule and move twice as fast while carrying it.

Wayne wasn't a bit surprised, but he was glad to have been proved right to others. Still, being a cautious man, he wanted to delay any general deployment of the animals for several years. During that time he planned to breed some large herds of domestic American camels, and before their deployment, he'd study the animals and learn how to better train them. And how to train men to work with them.

Secretary Davis disagreed with Wayne's plan. Things had gone just fine in Texas, and Davis insisted on immediate deployment of the camels in the service of the army. So in 1857, when Congress decided to establish a Federal Road from along the thirty-fifth parallel from El Paso to Fort Yuma on the Colorado River, the Camel Corps got its first job.

President James Buchanan appointed Lieutenant Edward Beale as head of the Camel Corps. His assignment was to survey a route for a wagon road from Fort Defiance to Fort Yuma, after first traveling to Fort Defiance from Camp Verde with the camels. If things went according to plan, a series of army posts would be set up along the route, which could be used for the transportation of mail and supplies.

And that was where Fargo came in. Beale was a friend of Kit Carson, and he'd asked Carson to go along as a scout on the Arizona to California leg of the expedition. Carson, however, was otherwise occupied. He had some family problems to deal with, and he suggested that the Trailsman take his place. Because Fargo had just finished guiding a party with Carson and was in the area, he was available. And he'd traveled in that part of the country before, something not many men could say.

"You'd better be careful if you take it on," Carson had told Fargo. "There's more to this than just some mapping expedition."

"How do you know?" Fargo asked.

"It's just a feeling. People have been hunting for treasure in this area for years, especially in the direction you're heading."

"You're talking about all that Spanish gold. Supposedly Coronado had it and hid it somewhere around there. I don't believe in it. People have told those stories ever since the Spanish passed this way, and nobody's ever found a thing."

"Because it's so well hidden," Carson said. "There are some caves along the route you're taking, maybe it's hidden there, out West." He laughed. "And maybe it's not. Anyway, you keep your eyes and ears open."

"I always do," Fargo told him.

Fargo had reservations after his talk with Carson, but he took the job. Now, however, he wasn't sure he'd have accepted, not if he'd known about the camels, which were likely to be a bigger source of trouble than any old tales of hidden gold. The camels had not been mentioned in his conversations with the army or with Carson, and Fargo had signed on to do the work as a scout before he even heard about them.

When he did hear, he was told only of their advantages, but in talking with some of the men on the post, he soon discovered that there were any number of drawbacks to the big animals.

They could be balky, they smelled terrible, their breath smelled even worse, and the mules, horses, and dogs hated them. And they spit. In addition to all that, they were temperamental, and learning to ride one was something Fargo wasn't willing to do. He didn't like the idea of being that far off the ground, and he didn't like the camel's gait. He mentioned all of that to Beale, who promised Fargo that he could ride his horse, a big Ovaro stallion.

Fargo had a certain amount of admiration for Beale, who, like Fargo, was an adventuresome sort and a man who'd accomplished a lot in his life so far. Kit Carson had told Fargo about how he and Beale had survived the battle of San Pasqual, in which a small American force had been surrounded by Mexican troops. In fact, Beale and Carson had slipped through the enemy lines and walked all the way to San Diego for reinforcements, thereby saving the American troops. And they'd had to walk part of the way without shoes, having been relieved of them by some Mexican troops they'd encountered along the way. Beale was tough and competent and not afraid of the devil.

So Fargo had agreed to help out, even after he found out about the camels.

Unfortunately, as soon as he'd satisfied himself about the job, he found out that the camels weren't the only complications involved.

"Women," Sergeant Carter had told him. "I just don't believe in lettin' women go along on an expedition like this one. You think them camels will be trouble? The women will be a hell of a lot more trouble than them camels, you mark my words."

Fargo didn't consider the women a problem, and he didn't mind having them along. He'd led expeditions that included women plenty of times, and more often than not they did as well as the men. In fact, they could be a positive benefit in more ways than one.

"It ain't the women I object to," Carter went on to explain. "I like women just as much as the next fella. It's the way the men behave around 'em that causes the trouble. You take a man who's been in the desert a while, away from what you might call civilizin' influences, and he's liable to do things that he oughtn't."

Fargo knew exactly what Carter meant, and the truth of the matter was that he wouldn't mind at all doing a few of those things with either of the women who'd be accompanying them—not that Fargo would ever have mentioned such a thing to Carter, who obviously wouldn't have approved.

The other problem, according to Carter, was Hi Jolly.

That wasn't his real name, but that's what everyone called him because it was as close as anybody could come to pronouncing his actual name, which was Hadji Ali. He was the camel driver, imported for the purpose, and he was the only one who'd had any lengthy experience with the animals.

Some of the soldiers had worked with them on the way from Texas, but even those who had still hadn't grown used to them. The soldiers were men who'd grown up riding horses. They were accustomed to the way horses behaved, and they could handle just about any problem with a horse just fine. A camel was an entirely different matter.

"They're sneaky bastards," Carter said. "They'll bite you if they think they can get away with it, and mostly they can. You gotta keep your eyes on 'em all the time, 'cause when they bite you, I can promise you that you'll know you've been bit."

"I'll let Hi Jolly handle the camels," Fargo said. "I'll keep my distance."

"I'm not sure I trust Hi Jolly any more than I do the camels," Carter told Fargo. "He's some kinda heathen. All the time prayin' to his heathen gods, bowing down and talkin' his heathen talk. He's worse than any Navajo I ever met, I can tell you that much. I wouldn't be surprised if he didn't slit all our throats one night while we're sleepin' and make off with the women and all our money."

"What money would that be?" Fargo asked.

"Well, I don't know, but somebody's bound to have some, and that heathen is likely to want it."

"What would he do with it?"

"He'd buy things. What the hell do you think money's for, Fargo, if it ain't to buy things? You can't eat it, you can't sleep with it, and it can't heal you if you're sick."

Fargo didn't have a good answer to that one, but he'd met Hi Jolly, and he didn't think the man was likely to slit anybody's throat. He seemed to care more about the camels than he did about money or anything else.

He was tall, lean, and swarthy, and he had a thick black moustache. He claimed that his mother was Greek and his father was Syrian, but no one knew for sure if that was true. No one was even sure where he'd come from. He'd just showed up when the camels were bought and volunteered to travel to America to help with them—for a fee, of course. One thing was for sure, he didn't look like anyone Fargo had ever seen before. He certainly didn't look like a fighter.

But, as Fargo knew, that didn't mean anything. He'd met plenty of men who looked completely harmless or even downright funny, but he'd discovered that there was nothing funny about the way they handled themselves in a fight.

It could be that Hi Jolly was the same, Fargo thought. He carried an oddly shaped, curved knife, and although Fargo had never seen him take it out of its scabbard, it might be deadly in a close fight. Come to think of it, the knife might even be sharp enough to slit a man's throat. Or a woman's.

"I'll be watchin' my back, is all I'm gonna say about it," Carter told Fargo. "You never know what might happen out there in the desert."

When Fargo thought about it later, he realized that Carter hadn't exaggerated one bit about the last part.

3

The trouble started the next day.

The camels were kept in a rectangular corral that had been built especially for them outside the fort. Instead of having a regular fence, it was surrounded by a wall higher than Fargo's head. He wasn't sure whether the wall was designed to keep the camels in or someone else out. As far as he knew, however, the Navajos hadn't seen the camels yet. He had a feeling that they wouldn't like them.

Fargo went to the corral at just about sunup with the Ovaro. The sun was turning the clouds in the east red and orange above the horizon, and it was going to be a warm day.

Fargo had been taking the horse out to the corral for the last couple of mornings to let it get acquainted with the camels. It had been skittish at first, but it was getting a little better now, though it hadn't exactly made friends with any of them.

As he led the horse along, Fargo saw Hi Jolly, who was performing his morning prayers. He was on some kind of rug or blanket and faced the East, but he didn't have any interest in the way the sun was tinting the low clouds. His eyes were closed, and his lips were moving as he spoke.

Fargo couldn't understand what Hi Jolly was saying, nor did he know the meanings of all the motions that Hi Jolly went through. These involved standing, sitting, crossing of arms over the chest, kneeling, and bowing, probably in an orderly sequence, though Fargo couldn't detect what it was. Carter had told Fargo that Hi Jolly performed these prayers something like four or five times a day.

"It's gonna be a real inconvenience on the trail, I can tell you that," Carter said. "Hi Jolly tells me he can't help it. He has to do it. I can't see Beale stoppin' the caravan for it, but maybe he will."

What was going to be an even greater inconvenience, Fargo was convinced, was that hardly anybody could ride a camel. Some of the soldiers would be on horseback, as would Fargo, but some would ride camels. And both the women insisted on riding the camels as well.

One of them, Sarah Gallagher, the sister of Randall Gallagher, the expedition's cartographer, was at the corral, ready for her camel-riding lesson, the last one before the expedition's departure the next day.

Fargo understood why a cartographer was necessary. Though he had mapped routes for new roads himself in the past, he was far from a professional, and he was glad that the government was providing someone to do that particular job. But he didn't know why Sarah had come along.

She was a beautiful young woman with corn silk yellow hair and blue eyes that could flash in anger or lighten in laughter, and she had a buxom figure that was hard to conceal even beneath the layers of clothing she typically wore.

This morning, however, she was dressed in men's denim pants and a hickory shirt and wearing a broadbrimmed hat. Fargo looked at her appreciatively as Hi Jolly rolled up his rug, and she smiled and waved to him.

"She is a beautiful woman," Hi Jolly said, standing beside Fargo with his rug tucked underneath his arm. He spoke pretty fair English, Fargo thought, better than some of the troopers.

"She is, for sure," Fargo agreed. "Are you going to teach her to ride a camel?"

"She has been learning. Today she will go for the first time outside the corral. You might want to observe, as you can learn for yourself how it is done."

Fargo didn't want to learn. He had no intention of ever sitting atop a camel. But he had no objections at all to watching Sarah Gallagher.

"I'll see how it goes," he said, and Hi Jolly went into the corral, smiling at Sarah as he passed her and inclining his head in a slight bow.

Fargo walked over to her and said, "Are you sure you want to ride a camel on this trip?"

"Why of course I am, Mr. Fargo. And why not? It's going to be a fine adventure, and the camels are just a part of it. We'll be mapping new territory for the government and traveling where no one has gone before."

"A wagon might be more comfortable."

"I'm not as interested in comfort as I am in adventure. I had to beg my brother for weeks to allow me to come with him, and then he had to plead with Lieutenant Beale. The lieutenant was reluctant. He didn't like the idea at all."

Fargo nodded, thinking of what Sergeant Carter had said about women.

"You're just like all the rest, aren't you?" Sarah said. "You don't think I belong here. You think all women are good for is cooking and cleaning and having babies."

Fargo thought nothing of the sort, but Sarah was getting worked up and didn't give him a chance to say anything.

"You think women are weak and stupid and inferior. Well, Mr. Fargo, I'll have you know that I'm as smart as any man. I've been to school, even to college, and I'm not weak. You'll see. I'll be as strong as any man on this expedition. My brother had to threaten not to come if I wasn't allowed, but I'll prove my mettle."

Fargo said that he didn't doubt it. He also wanted to say that Sarah Gallagher was beautiful when her blue eyes sparked with anger and the red coloring rose to her cheeks, but he knew better than to do that right at the moment.

"I know there'll be danger," Sarah said, "but I'm not afraid. We're exploring unknown territory, but I'm not one bit intimidated. On the contrary. I'm excited."

"The country's not exactly unknown," Fargo pointed out. "You're forgetting about the Navajos. I expect they've been just about everywhere around here."

Her anger disappeared as quickly as it had come, and she gave him a dazzling smile.

"Well, of course they have. But they didn't make any maps, now did they? So as far as we're concerned, it's totally unexplored."

That was close enough to the truth, and Fargo wasn't in any mood to argue. He seldom was when he was around a pretty woman, even one who was as attractive as this one when her temper got the upper hand. At least now he knew why she had come along, and he couldn't blame her for it.

Sarah was about to say something more, but Hi Jolly came out of the corral leading a camel. Fargo felt the Ovaro quiver beside him—not much, about the way he would have if he'd been wrinkling his hide to get rid of a pesky fly. It was enough to let Fargo know that the horse wasn't completely comfortable around camels yet.

"They do have a powerful smell, don't they," Sarah said as the camel approached, and Fargo had to agree. It was a stink unlike anything else he'd ever smelled. He didn't think he was likely to get used to it, no matter how long they were on the trail.

The camel that Hi Jolly led was a male, a little smaller than some of the others, but a male nevertheless. Fargo knew this without having to look because he'd been told that all the camels to be used on the expedition were males. It didn't work to take females out along with males. Camels behaved like Carter claimed soldiers did, only worse, and having females along would cause far too many complications. Fargo considered mentioning this fact to Sarah, but he thought better of it.

Though the camel was a bit smaller than average, it still had a high-humped back, higher than Fargo's head by a good way. Fargo had heard that some camels had two humps, but he'd never seen one like that, and he didn't care if he ever did. Besides the hump, this one had thick lips, long eyelashes, and broad feet. Its long lower lip hung down, making the camel look as if he were brooding over some serious problem. There were callouses on its knees, but it seemed to have more knees that it should. It wasn't built like any animal he was accustomed to being around. Its front legs bent in a kind of Z-shape, and the back legs bent in something more like an *S*.

17

Hi Jolly had saddled the animal, if you could call the thing sitting atop it a saddle. It didn't look much like a saddle to Fargo. It had a high pommel and a high cantle, both of which stuck out at an angle. It rested on several cloths on the animal's shoulders in front of its hump and had something like a blanket thrown over it. The bridle looked more like a hackamore than anything else, and Hi Jolly held it tightly.

He stopped in front of Sarah and handed the rope to her.

"You have done this before," he said. "Remember that you must be firm. Camels do not understand gentleness."

"I remember," Sarah said, taking the rope.

When she had a good grip on it, she cleared her throat loudly. The camel looked off into the distance, as if it had heard nothing at all.

Sarah cleared her throat again, more loudly than before and gave a hard pull on the rope.

This time the camel paid attention. Moaning as if it was in pain, it started to kneel. Then it thought better of it and tried to stand again. Sarah cleared her throat and jerked the rope.

The camel groaned, stretched out its long, flexible neck, and made a loud and disgusting gurgling noise, but Sarah ignored it, and it finally started down again. It knelt on its front knees, folded its back legs up, and then at the last it tucked the rest of its front legs under its belly.

The Ovaro snorted, not loudly, but loud enough to suggest that even he was amazed at the unnatural abilities of the camel.

When the animal was finally on the ground, Fargo watched as Sarah walked to its side. She kept a strong grip on the rope and pulled the camel's head around toward its shoulder. The camel allowed its head to move, but very reluctantly. Sarah didn't seem to notice. She kept right on pulling, and eventually she had her way. When the camel's head was firmly jammed into its body, Sara was ready to mount.

"Now is the time of greatest danger," Hi Jolly whispered to Fargo. The camel driver's body was tense. "If

18

she should release his head before she throws her leg over the saddle, he will run away and throw her to the ground."

But Fargo could tell that the camel wouldn't get a chance to do anything like that. Sarah kept the rope taut and kept the camel's head pressed firmly into its body until she had seated herself in the uncomfortable-looking saddle.

Hi Jolly relaxed. "Remember to grip the camel's body with your knees and continue to hold tightly to the rope."

"I remember," Sarah said without looking in Hi Jolly's direction.

"Very well. Now you can give him his head."

When Sarah did so, the camel began to rise, unfolding those incredible legs, and Fargo saw the necessity of the high pommel on the saddle and the tight grip with the knees. The camel rose on its long back legs first, and an unwary rider could easily have been thrown forward over its head if it had risen with unexpected speed.

The camel, which hadn't wanted to kneel in the first place, now didn't seem any happier to be getting up. It moaned as if it were undergoing some kind of terrible torture, but Sarah kept her grip and waited until it finally reached its feet.

Sarah sat high above the ground, swaying slightly in the saddle and smiling down at Hi Jolly and Fargo as if she had accomplished something special.

Fargo supposed that in a way she had. It certainly wasn't anything he'd want to do. He'd heard about the great loads camels could carry without tiring and of their ability to go without water for days on end, up to a week if necessary, so he supposed they would be fine for work animals. But he wondered if riding one of them was worth all the trouble.

"You can let him walk now," Hi Jolly told Sarah.

Sarah moved her legs in front of the saddle and rested them on the slope of the camel's shoulders, as the saddle had no stirrups. When she was comfortable, she gently urged the camel forward.

The way the big animal walked was another thing Fargo didn't like. It lifted the two feet on the right side of its body at the same time, took a step, and then lifted the two feet on the left side for the next step. It continued like that, with a rocking, swaying motion that a sailor might have liked. Fargo, however, thought he might get seasick just watching.

The rocking motion didn't seem to bother Sarah in the least, and everything was going well until she decided to encourage the camel to go a little faster.

At first Fargo thought the camel would refuse to obey, being a contrary beast, but this time it chose to do what Sarah had asked and to cause trouble by obeying rather than by refusing.

It sped up, slowly at first, and then gained speed gradually until it was running full out, an awesome sight. Sarah was being tossed about now like a sailor in a gale.

Although the camel appeared awkward and ungainly, and while the rider's position seemed tenuous at best, Fargo thought that a race between a camel and a horse would be mighty interesting to see.

"He will not kill her," Hi Jolly said at Fargo's side, reminding him that horse racing wasn't the thing to be thinking about right at the moment. "At least I hope he will not."

"What are you talking about?" Fargo asked.

"It is sometimes easy to get a camel to run," Hi Jolly said. "It is not always quite so easy to get him to stop."

"Can't she just pull back on the rope?"

"She can do that. I hope she will. But that might not bother the camel. A camel is a stubborn beast. Sometimes it will run until it falls. And if it falls . . ."

"Then it will fall on Miss Gallagher," Fargo said.

"Exactly. Or, if it does not fall . . ."

"It'll throw her off."

"You are correct again, Mr. Fargo."

Fargo looked at the Ovaro. No saddle. Only a bridle. A Navajo might be able to make a ride of it. Fargo figured he could, too.

And he had to try. There was nobody else around.

He took hold of the bridle and jumped up on the Ovaro's back. When he was settled, he leaned low over the horse's neck, put his heels to the its sides, and said, "Let's have us that race."

20

4

The Ovaro fairly flew over the ground, and Fargo struggled to hang on, not being used to riding bareback. His knees gripped the horse's sides as tightly as Sarah's must have gripped the camel.

Fargo was bounced around a bit on the Ovaro's broad back, but he was as comfortable as an old man in a rocking chair compared to Sarah, who appeared to be barely hanging on to the pommel of her saddle with one hand. With the other she was pulling back on the rope as if trying to break the camel's neck. The camel didn't seem to notice.

Fargo realized that he and the Ovaro weren't gaining on the camel. If anything, they were dropping behind.

He also realized that if the camel stumbled, or if the Ovaro did, the animals and their riders were going to be in serious trouble.

He had to give Sarah credit for her efforts. She was struggling, but she was far from giving up. Fargo saw her mouth working, and he thought she was yelling at the camel, but he couldn't hear the words.

Sarah had hauled back so hard on the rope that the camel's head was nearly touching the pommel of the saddle, but still the big animal careened forward. The Ovaro was strained to the limit, but it was unable to gain any ground.

Then something happened to change things. Fargo wasn't sure what it was at first, but he was now gaining ground on the camel, or rather the camel was no longer heading away from him. It appeared to have turned around and started back where it had come from.

But Fargo soon realized that wasn't the case. Instead of having turned completely around, the camel had begun to make a large circle. With its head pulled into its shoulder, it was no longer able, or at least willing, to run straight ahead.

Fargo thought at first this was because the camel couldn't see what was in front of it, but that couldn't have been the reason. After all, it couldn't see much of anything at all, considering the position of its head, yet it continued to run in a wide ring and didn't appear to have any intention of stopping any time soon. It had hardly even slowed down.

But maybe that didn't matter. If it wasn't going to stop or slow down, it wasn't going anywhere, either. And if Sarah could stay in the saddle for a while, Fargo had a chance to reach her. The Ovaro wouldn't even have to chase the camel. Fargo could just stay in one place on the circumference of the circle and wait for the camel to come to him.

Fargo maneuvered the Ovaro into position and pulled back on the bridle. The big horse stopped, and Fargo eyed the camel. It was about halfway through its loop, and Sarah was still hanging on to both the rope and the pommel. Fargo saw that she had whipped the rope around the pommel, making sure that the camel's head wasn't going to move back around to the front.

The camel's wide, two-toed feet sent up clouds of dust with every rocking step as it pounded along its new route. With its head twisted back, it looked almost like a moving rock with legs.

As Sarah got closer to him, Fargo could hear what she was saying. The names she was calling the camel would have done an imaginative mule skinner proud.

The camel didn't hear them, or, more likely, didn't care what she was calling him. It kept right on going in its circle, taking its strange strides and rolling Sarah from side to side as it rambled along.

When the camel had nearly reached him, Fargo guided the Ovaro into its own circle, and the horse ran alongside the camel.

"You sorry sack of sheep shit!" Sarah yelled at the animal. "Stop right now!"

She pulled back on the rope, but the camel's head was already turned as far as it was going to.

Fargo reached out an arm.

"Slide over," he said to Sarah. "I'll take you off."

Sarah looked at him, and her blue eyes flashed.

"I'm not going to get off. I'll ride him until he drops dead, the bastard."

Fargo wondered if she was toning down her language because she knew he could hear her now. He said, "Lieutenant Beale wouldn't like that. He's going to need all the camels for the trip. You'd better not kill one of them."

They rode along for several more yards. With the camel going around in a ring, the Ovaro was finding it easy to keep up.

"I've heard camels can go on for days without food or water," Fargo said. "But I don't think you can."

After she'd thought that over, Sarah said, "Oh, all right." But Fargo could tell she didn't relish the idea of having him put his hands on her.

She unwound the rope from around the pommel, though still keeping her grip on it. Then she slid off the saddle into Fargo's waiting arm, at the same time throwing one leg over the Ovaro's back and letting go of the rope. As soon as the camel detected the slack, its neck snaked back to its normal position. Almost as soon as Sarah was settled atop the Ovaro behind Fargo, the camel started back toward the spot where Hi Jolly stood. It had not gone far before it began to slow down, and by the time it had gone fifty yards, it was walking.

"If that camel thinks I'm not going to ride it when we leave here tomorrow, it has another think coming," Sarah said.

Fargo was conscious of her firm breasts pressing into his back as they rode along behind the camel, though it was obvious that she was trying to avoid the contact. He thought about suggesting that she ride with him instead of on the camel. But he knew better than to put the thought into words.

"You didn't have to rescue me, you know," Sarah said. "Sooner or later that stupid beast would have real-

23

ized that I wasn't going to give up. Then it would have stopped its misbehaving."

Fargo wasn't so sure. The more he saw of the camels in action, the less he liked them, and the more certain he was that misbehaving was part of their character.

"He might just have fallen down and rolled over on you," he said. "Then you'd have a broken leg, or worse, and you'd have to stay behind at the fort while the rest of us went on the expedition. You wouldn't have liked that, would you?"

"No, but I don't believe it would have happened that way. Men always seem to think a woman can't take care of herself, but they're dead wrong."

"I've known plenty of women who could take care of themselves," Fargo told her, even though her comment had sounded oddly unconvincing.

Sarah was silent for a few seconds, and Fargo thought her arms tightened around him just a little. But maybe it was just his imagination, because if it had happened at all, she immediately drew back.

"I'll just bet you have," Sarah said.

Fargo thought the conversation was about to get interesting, but by that time they had reached Hi Jolly, who stood waiting for them, holding the rope attached to Sarah's camel, which was now standing docilely and chewing its cud with a loud, sloppy eating noise.

"I most humbly apologize," Hi Jolly said when Sarah slipped off the Ovaro beside him. "I had no idea that the stupid camel would run away like that. It was my fault, and I abase myself before you. My regrets are so many that they outnumber the grains of sand in the desert. I must humble myself to you and beg that you accept my apologies."

"Oh, stop it, Hi Jolly," Sarah said. "It wasn't your fault, and there's no need for you to carry on about it. I was the one who tried to get the camel to run, and it did. It just did a little more than I asked for."

Seeing that he wasn't being blamed for the camel's behavior, Hi Jolly switched instantly from being contrite and subservient to condemning and accusatory.

"You should never try the camel's patience and never

encourage it to run. A woman is not capable of riding in those circumstances. I have said as much to Lieutenant Beale, but he refuses to listen to me. He believes the camel to be a noble beast, such that even a woman cannot ruin its qualities, but I, Hadji Ali, who have lived in the desert and seen the treatment that the brute requires, know better. But will anyone listen to me? No. I am the camel driver, hired because of my years of experience, but no one will take my advice, and so you are nearly killed and the camel is nearly rendered useless to the expedition. You shall not ride the camels again. I, Hadji Ali, have said so."

There was an ominous silence while Sarah stared at Hi Jolly. Her face had grown red as he was talking, and Fargo thought she might slap the camel driver.

But she didn't. Instead, she broke into laughter.

"You're wonderful, Hi Jolly," she said when she was able. "I appreciate your concern for your camels and for my safety. And for the safety of the expedition. But you don't have to worry about me. I won't let that camel run away with me again. What is its name?"

"It does not have a name," Hi Jolly said, maintaining his dignity in the face of Sarah's laughter. "It is merely a camel."

"Then I'm going to call it Samuel," Sarah said. "Because it reminds me of someone I once knew."

"A man who wouldn't do what you told him?" Fargo said.

Sarah turned and gave him a searching look.

"Men usually do what I tell them," she said. "And when they don't, I stretch their necks."

Fargo didn't doubt it. He didn't envy Samuel, whoever he was.

"I must put the camel back in the *kraal*," Hi Jolly said.

"Samuel," Sarah said. "Please use his name."

Hi Jolly did not respond. He led the camel away.

"He must not have heard you," Fargo said.

"Oh, he heard me, all right. I'm afraid that in Hi Jolly's culture women have very little to say, and even on those rare occasions when they are allowed to talk, no one listens to them. Hi Jolly isn't at all accustomed to having a woman speak up to him, and it goes against his grain." She gave Fargo another look. "How about your grain, Fargo?"

"When somebody talks, I always listen," Fargo said. "Man or woman, makes no difference to me. If you have something you want to say, you can go right ahead."

"We'll see," Sarah told him.

She turned away from him and walked back toward the fort. Fargo watched the way her hips moved in the mannish pants she wore and thought that it was going to be a very interesting trip to California.

5

That night after the evening meal, Lieutenant Beale held a meeting of all those who would be leaving for California the next morning.

He was a handsome man with a straight nose and a thick brown moustache. He stood with his back straight and his hands clasped behind him.

"First of all, I want to impress upon all of you the importance of our mission," he said. "Not just the road that we will be mapping along the thirty-fifth parallel, although that is quite important. But there is also our mission to prove the value of the camel as a beast of burden for the American continent. It is my belief that the harder the test we put the animals to, the better they will respond. Some of you have come with me from Texas, and you have seen what they can do.

"But those of you who are joining the expedition at this time will be amazed at the abilities of the camels. They can haul tremendous burdens of hay and oats without receiving a grain of their load to eat, living for the most part on greasewood and shrubbery. They can walk for days under the blazing sun without drinking a drop of water. I look forward to the time when every mail route in the country will be worked by these wonderful beasts, and this expedition will be the beginning of that process."

He went on in that vein for several minutes, and Fargo's mind drifted. He didn't need to be sold on the camels. No matter what happened on the trip to California, and no matter how well the camels responded, Fargo was never going to ride one of them. Whatever the shortcomings of a horse might be in comparison,

Fargo preferred to stick to an animal he knew and understood to learning about one that appeared to be the offspring of the devil.

So instead of listening to Beale, Fargo looked around the dining hall at the people he'd be traveling with for the next few weeks.

His eye lit first on Randall Gallagher. The cartographer was a strongly built man but short, shorter than his sister and much thicker through the body. His hair was a darker blond than hers, and his eyes were brown instead of blue. The wrinkles at the corners of his eyes testified to the time he'd spent outdoors in the sun, and his big hands looked more like the hands of a stonecutter than a mapmaker. Fargo had talked to him a bit, however, and knew that he was good at what he did.

Fargo hardly had to look at Sergeant Carter to know that the man would rather be out on the trail than in some room listening to a speech. Fargo felt he knew Carter better than any of the others, and if there was any trouble on the trail, Carter was the man Fargo would turn to for help.

Troopers Wayne Logan and John Slater were likely to be sources of trouble, Fargo knew, just as they had been during the recent race, and he glanced around until he saw them, both of them leaning back in their chairs, their eyes half closed, appearing almost asleep as Beale's voice droned on.

They weren't disrespectful, Fargo supposed, but they weren't far from it. They would be the kind who were always right on the edge of insolence, and sooner or later they'd cross the line.

Fargo didn't know the other soldiers well at all. There was a corporal named Vinson who seemed competent, and Fargo had seen him with the camels. He could handle them better than anyone other than Hi Jolly, who sat quietly, listening to Beale as if hanging on every word. Fargo doubted that he was. That morning, Hi Jolly had revealed himself to be a bit insecure in his own position, while at the same time being protective of his authority, such as it was. Fargo thought that he'd have to keep an eye on the camel driver.

Troopers Rollins, Temple, Taylor, and Spence were

among the others whom Fargo had met. They seemed interested enough in what was going on, but he didn't think they were happy about working with the camels. They hadn't demonstrated any enthusiasm for the animals during the times Fargo had been with them.

The other woman who'd be going along was Jane Montgomery, the daughter of Robert Montgomery, one of the expedition's two civilian surveyors. She, like Sarah Gallagher, had insisted on being allowed to travel on the expedition. She was another one with a desire for adventure, Fargo supposed, though she had been on other surveying trips and might simply have thought it was only natural for a daughter to travel with her father when she had the chance.

There were several other civilians along as well. Clyde Johnson was the other surveyor, and Henry Tolliver was both a botanist and a doctor. Fargo hoped they wouldn't have any need of his doctoring skills, but you could never tell when a man like that would come in handy. Tolliver wore a sola topee, a hard domed sun hat of the kind that Fargo had heretofore seen only on a couple of British explorers he'd met.

Franklin Biggle, a short man with wire-rimmed glasses, was a geologist and mining engineer. There weren't any mines along the route, and Fargo wondered why Biggle was part of the group. Maybe there was something to the gold talk, after all. If there was, things could get awkward in a hurry. Gold had a way of causing a lot of complications. More likely, Biggle was along to study rock formations, something that held no interest for Fargo.

What could prove even more awkward than Spanish gold was the presence of Miss Montgomery. She was about thirty, Fargo judged, and a beautiful woman. Unlike Sarah, Jane was a brunette with hair as black as the prairie sky at night. While she was not as voluptuous as Sarah, her slim figure was no less attractive.

Her father looked stooped and tired, and Fargo wondered what the man was doing there. He'd been a last-minute substitution for the original surveyor, who'd had some kind of accident in New Mexico on his way to Fort Defiance. Montgomery had been in New Mexico as well, and not too far away, and he'd volunteered his services. Fargo hoped he wouldn't be a problem on the trail.

Jane, in stark comparison to her father, looked as fresh as a flower, and that was likely to present complications of another kind, what with all the men around. Sergeant Carter had been right about that, no matter what Sarah Gallagher might have to say on the subject.

Beale finished his speech, assuring everyone once again that camels would be a big part of the future of the country. Fargo caught Sarah Gallagher's eye and gave her a questioning look, as if to ask if she agreed. She smiled and nodded. Fargo could tell that her experience with Samuel that morning hadn't discouraged her.

It was, Fargo thought, going to be a very interesting trip, through country that, if not exactly hostile, wasn't the most inviting that he'd ever traveled. He wasn't sure he was looking forward to it.

The noise that greeted Fargo the next morning just after dawn was unlike anything he'd ever heard, though he had a feeling he'd be hearing it often in the days to come. It was the sound of all the camels together protesting the fact that they were being loaded down with their packs for the day's travel. It sounded as if someone had stirred up all the demons of the desert.

"Sorry-soundin' bastards, ain't they?" Sergeant Carter said.

He and Fargo stood outside the corral, both of them reluctant to go inside.

"One of 'em spit on me once," Carter went on. "It wasn't as bad as some things I've had on me, I guess, but it was bad enough. Slicker'n owl shit. I thought I'd never get it off. You had breakfast yet?"

Fargo said he had.

"Don't know why I thought of breakfast. That camel spit sure didn't remind me of it. Anyhow, I'd rather eat than say a bunch of prayers like Hi Jolly. You see him this mornin'?"

Fargo told Carter that he had indeed seen the camel driver. He had been at his prayers when Fargo went to breakfast in the mess hall.

"All that prayin' might be good for him, but it seems

like a lot of work to me. You think that Gallagher woman is really gonna ride one of them camels?"

Fargo said he believed that was the plan and suggested that they could go inside the corral and find out.

"I'd just as soon not have to face those sons of bitches this early in the mornin'," Carter said. "But I guess I have to see 'em sooner or later. Let's go."

They went through the gates, and the sight that greeted them was equal to the noise they'd heard outside. The camels that were loaded refused to get up. The ones that were not yet burdened refused to kneel. And every one of them was bellowing.

Hi Jolly was there, going from camel to camel to help the man who was working with it. He would strike the animals behind the knees with a hard, short stick, and that worked some of the time to get them to kneel. Some of the time it didn't.

"Rather have a mule any day of the week," Carter said. "They can be stubborn sons of bitches, but I never seen nothin' like this before."

Fargo hadn't either, but he figured he might as well get used to it. Near one wall of the enclosure, he saw Sarah Gallagher talking to Jane Montgomery, whose dark hair and eyes made her quite a contrast to Sarah's blondness. While Fargo watched, Jane put on a wide-brimmed hat designed to protect her from the sun. She wore her long hair in a thick braid that hung down her back almost to her waist.

As far as Fargo knew, Jane wasn't planning to ride a camel. Only Sarah and a few of the troopers, and of course Lieutenant Beale, planned to do that. Most of the animals were reserved for carrying their heavy loads of supplies and equipment.

"I believe I'll go talk to Miss Gallagher," Fargo told Carter.

Carter gave him a crooked grin. "Don't blame you none. I'd do the same if I thought I could spare the time. She's a hell of a lot prettier than those damn camels. But I need to see to the troops. The ones that are new to it don't seem to be gettin' the hang of things, much as they've tried."

Fargo was of the opinion that they hadn't tried very hard, but he kept his thought to himself. They'd have plenty of time to practice once they got on the trail. It was too bad that some of the more experienced men were being left behind at Fort Defiance, but Beale's idea was that the trip to Fort Yuma would be a good opportunity to train more men in the use of the camels. Fargo wasn't sure it was such a good idea, especially since the new men included Logan and Slater.

Carter went to help out with the camels, and Fargo walked over to where the women stood. The smell of the camels was so powerful that he had to restrain an urge to cover his nose.

"It's terrible, isn't it?" Jane Montgomery said.

"What is?" Fargo said.

She laughed. "The smell. Why else would your face have such a look on it?"

"Mr. Fargo is of the opinion that women shouldn't have anything to do with camels," Sarah said. "Maybe that's the cause of his unhappy look."

"No," Fargo said. "It's the smell, all right. And what makes you think I have anything against women riding camels?"

"You've tried to dissuade me often enough. In the meantime, I've been telling Jane what a wonderful experience it is, and I've suggested that she give it a try."

There was a wicked glint in Sarah's eye, and Fargo wondered if there was something between the two of them that he didn't know about. More than likely, he told himself, it was just the natural competition of two beautiful women. If Sarah was going to look foolish on camelback, she might not want to be alone. Or maybe she knew she was going to do just fine but wouldn't mind seeing Jane embarrassed if the other woman proved a poor rider. Either way, it was just one more complication as far as Fargo could tell.

"I don't believe I'd do very well at riding a camel," Jane said in her smoky voice. "There are other things that I'm much better at riding."

She looked at Fargo from under the brim of her hat when she said it, and he wondered exactly what she meant. If he was lucky, he might get a chance to find out before they got to California.

"I'm sure you're an expert," Sarah said. "I wonder if you're as good as I am."

Fargo was beginning to believe that the expedition held a lot more promise than he'd first thought, and that competition between two women, while it might be an occasionally troublesome complication, certainly had its good points.

While he was considering the possibilities, Hi Jolly came over to them and said, "It is time for you to get ready to ride, Miss Gallagher. If you will follow me, please."

He didn't look happy, and Fargo didn't blame him. There was enough trouble with the camels already without him having to deal with getting Sarah on one of them.

But Sarah didn't seem to think so. She smiled and followed Hi Jolly, turning back to wave at Fargo as she went.

"I heard someone say you had to rescue her yesterday," Jane said when Sarah was out of earshot. "Do you think she's capable of taking care of herself?"

"I'm sure she is. I didn't have to rescue her, exactly. Just help her out a little. How about you? Can you take care of yourself?"

"I sometimes need a bit of help. My father and I will be in a wagon, though, so I don't think I'll need rescuing."

"If you do," Fargo said, "I'll do what I can."

"I'm sure you will. Now if you'll excuse me, I'd better go find my father."

She left the corral, and Fargo thought it might be time for him to go, too. He had to saddle the Ovaro, though he knew he could be finished with that job long before all the camels were loaded and ready to leave.

On his way outside, he passed by Lieutenant Beale, who stopped him with a hand on his arm.

"The camels are magnificent, aren't they, Fargo?" Beale said.

"They're something, for sure," Fargo said, being careful not to define *something*.

Beale watched the animals with satisfaction, not seeming to notice the difficulties that the men were having. Fargo had to admit that things were going a little better now than they had been earlier. Several of the camels were

33

loaded and on their feet, and most of the others seemed to have resigned themselves to having to go to work.

"Do you foresee any dangers ahead of us?" Beale asked.

"Do you mean the terrain?"

"Yes. And anything else, of course."

"Well, you know I've traveled in this part of the country before," Fargo said. "From what I've seen of it, it's not as bad as a lot of other places. Horses and mules can do just fine."

Beale nodded with satisfaction. "Then camels should do even better. And what about other things?"

The other things weren't really a part of Fargo's job. He was just a guide. But he'd been worrying ever since the horse race about one thing in particular.

"I wonder about Manuelito," he said.

"What about him?"

"You heard about the horse race, I guess."

"I heard about it. A regrettable incident, but nothing to cause undue alarm, surely."

"I don't know about that," Fargo said. "Short Knife was the man who was cheated in the race, and he's Manuelito's cousin. Manuelito might take it personally."

"I was told that what happened in the race was an accident."

"That's what the soldiers involved in it said," Fargo told him. "But it wasn't. It was deliberate cheating, and everybody knows that. Especially the Indians."

"I see. And when do you think Manuelito will attack? Assuming, of course, that he does."

"He'll wait until after we're well away from the fort, so it won't be on the first day. Maybe the second. He might even wait until the third."

"And after that?" Beale said.

"If he hasn't attacked by then, we're in the clear. He won't stray that far away from here just to satisfy his pride."

Beale rubbed his chin and ran a finger over his moustache.

"Are you a gambling man, Fargo?"

"I've laid down a card or two now and then. Bet on a horse occasionally. But not the other day."

34

"And if you were betting, what would you say the chances are that we'll get through the next three days without a visit from Manuelito."

"If I was betting," Fargo told him, "I'd say there was just about next to no chance at all."

"That's what I think, too, now that you've explained the circumstances," Beale said. "But we didn't expect this trip to be easy, did we?"

"No," Fargo said. "We sure didn't."

By the time Fargo had the Ovaro saddled and ready to go, the camels were moving out of the corral. Fargo had to admit that it was an impressive sight. The big animals ambled along in a line, stringing out along the trail, most of them carrying loads that would cripple the strongest mule ever born. And they didn't even seem too much bothered by them. After all their complaining, they weren't overly burdened. They had objected only because that was their nature.

Sarah Gallagher sat swaying atop the camel she'd named Samuel, and she gave Fargo another wave as she rode past him. He touched the brim of his hat and smiled.

After the camels came the wagons with the civilians, and the troopers rode behind. But Fargo didn't want to see them. He put his heels to the Ovaro's side and galloped along beside the caravan until he had passed the lead camel. Hi Jolly was sitting on it, looking as comfortable as a man relaxing in his favorite rocking chair.

Fargo slowed and rode alongside Hi Jolly for a minute and asked him if everything he'd seen that morning was the usual behavior of camels.

"It is," Hi Jolly said. "Things will go faster when the inexperienced men get more used to them."

"I hope so," Fargo said, meaning it. It was now well after sunup, and he'd hoped to be on his way somewhat earlier.

"You will see," Hi Jolly said. "Everything will be fine. This will be a good experience for you. You will grow to appreciate the camels for all their fine qualities."

"Yeah," Fargo said. "I'm sure that's right."

But he didn't believe it for a minute.

35

6

The first hint of trouble came at noon.

It didn't come from Manuelito and the Navajos. It came instead from the troopers themselves. Or from some of them. Fargo had more or less expected it.

Up until that time, however, things had gone well. The camels were everything Fargo could have hoped for: sure-footed, tireless, and amiable. Fargo decided that after they finally got on their feet and started down the trail, they were fine. Getting them started was the hard part. The wagons had a bit of difficulty in some places, but not the camels.

The big animals chewed their cuds noisily and gave out with an occasional bawl for reasons that no one could determine, but they didn't slow down. Their wide, two-toed feet, which looked funny to anyone used to a horse or a mule, were perfect for the desert terrain. Fargo had thought that rocks might present some difficulties because the bottoms of the camels' feet appeared to be soft, but the rocks didn't seem to hurt them. Maybe, Fargo thought, Beale was right about them. Maybe they would be taking over every mail route in the country.

There was no doubt that the camels wouldn't have any need to stop at noon, but the horses and the humans needed a rest. When Fargo came to a place that had some high rocks to provide shelter from the sun, he rode back to Beale and suggested that they stop there. Beale told Carter to give the word to Hi Jolly and the troopers.

After the column came to a halt, Hi Jolly said that it would be best if the camels were kept standing. Once they knelt to rest, it would be hard to get them back up.

So only the camels that were carrying riders were allowed to kneel down, and they were reluctant. There was more bellowing and roaring.

Once Beale dismounted and was on solid ground, he walked down the column, congratulating the men on their so-far successful trip, talking to the civilians about their jobs, and telling Hi Jolly that he could perform his prayers if he saw fit.

Hi Jolly was ready to pray, but only after he had checked on the camels. When he was satisfied that they were all fine, he went off out of sight of the others to do his praying.

Biggle was off looking at rocks, sometimes knocking a hunk off one or another of them with a hammer that he carried and peering at them through his glasses. Occasionally he would save a sample in a small pouch that hung from his belt.

There weren't many plants for Henry Tolliver to examine, but he drew pictures in his notebook of those that he found and wrote careful notes about them. He appeared odd and out of place to Fargo as he stood there in his funny-looking helmet.

The column had made two brief stops along the way for the surveyors, and now Montgomery and Johnson set up their instruments for more measurements. Fargo thought that Montgomery already looked the worse for wear after only a half day's travel, and he walked over to see if the man was all right. His daughter arrived at about the same time Fargo did.

"How are you feeling?" she asked Montgomery.

The surveyor straightened and said, "I'm fine, my dear. Clyde is seeing that I don't overdo things."

"That's right," Clyde Johnson said. "We have a long way to go, and we need to conserve our energy."

Johnson was a cheerful young man with chiseled features and a determined look. Jane seemed to like him, and she thanked him for any help he could give her father.

"You're babying me," Montgomery told his daughter. "You know how I hate that."

"Someone has to look after you," Jane said. "You know you try too hard to keep up with younger men."

Montgomery looked at her with his watery brown eyes. "I'm not as old as I seem to be. Someday you'll understand that the years don't change a man as much as young people think, not on the inside."

"All the same, you take it easy. I don't want Dr. Tolliver to have to take you on as a patient."

"Don't worry about me. I'll be fine. Come along, Johnson. Let's get to work."

The surveyors turned to their instruments, and Montgomery seemed spry enough. Fargo didn't worry about him. He was looking forward to having Jane to himself for a while. But before he could even begin to talk, he heard the sound of a cry from beyond the rocks.

"That sounded like Sarah," Jane said, but Fargo was already on his way to see what the trouble was.

On the other side of the rocks, Fargo found Logan holding Sarah's wrist as she fought to break his grip and get at Slater, who was tormenting Hi Jolly by tugging at the edge of his prayer rug as if to jerk it from beneath his knees.

"Stop it!" Sarah said. "You have no right to interrupt him when he's praying."

"Praying?" Logan said. "I don't know that I'd call it that. You can't even understand what he's saying."

Slater gave another jerk at the prayer rug, but Hi Jolly kept right on with the incomprehensible prayers.

"Let Miss Gallagher go," Fargo told Logan.

Logan glanced around and saw Fargo for the first time. He laughed.

"You can't give me orders, Fargo. You don't have the authority."

"That's right, civilian," Slater said, giving Hi Jolly a kick in the rump.

Hi Jolly rocked forward, but he refused to topple over, and the stream of his prayers never stopped flowing. Slater drew back his leg for a harder kick, and Fargo pulled his big .45 from its holster.

"I might be a civilian," Fargo said, "but I can still fill you full of holes. Now get away from Hi Jolly."

"Seems like you're always interfering in things that are none of your business, Fargo," Logan said.

Fargo turned the pistol so that it pointed over Sarah's shoulder at Logan's head.

"Yeah, I guess I am," Fargo said. "So while we're at it, you can let go of Miss Gallagher."

"You can kiss my ass," Logan said.

Fargo pulled back the hammer of the .45.

"You can't shoot," Logan said. "You might hit Miss Gallagher."

The way he said *miss* made it sound like something nasty, and Fargo was tempted to shoot him just for that. He might have done it, too, if Slater hadn't thrown a rock and hit him in the shoulder.

When the rock hit Fargo, Logan shoved Sarah at him as hard as he could. She stumbled into Fargo, throwing him farther off balance.

Before he could recover, Slater grabbed his wrist and twisted. Logan threw Sarah to the ground, then slugged Fargo in the stomach with a hard right fist. Before he could hit him again Fargo kicked the soldier in the crotch.

Logan sank down, clutching himself and moaning. Drool ran out of his mouth.

"Bastard," Slater said.

He let go of Fargo's wrist and grabbed the .45. Fargo held on to the pistol, and when Slater pulled on it, the gun fired. The bullet whanged off a rock, sending stone splinters flying.

Surprised, Slater jumped backward, and Fargo leveled the pistol on him.

"If you move, I'll shoot your knee," Fargo said. "Dr. Tolliver might save your leg, but you'll never walk without a limp again."

Slater straightened up, glaring at Fargo.

"See about Miss Gallagher," Fargo said.

"What about Logan?"

Logan was rocking and moaning, with his hands between his legs.

"I don't give a damn about Logan," Fargo said. He saw that Sarah was sitting up and watching them. "But you can have him. Get him out of here."

Slater went to Logan and tried to help him to his feet, but Logan wasn't going to be getting up for a while.

People had started to show up to see what the shoot-ing was all about. Fargo said that there'd been a little misunderstanding.

"But it's all taken care of now. These men thought they could have a little fun with Hi Jolly. Miss Gallagher and I put a stop to it."

"It won't happen again," Lieutenant Beale said, look-ing at Slater. "Isn't that right?"

"Yes, sir," Slater said. "I'm sorry, sir."

"What about Logan?"

"Fargo kicked him, sir. He can't talk right now."

If Slater thought his comment would get Fargo in trouble, he was wrong.

"I'm sure he deserved kicking," Beale said.

"He'll have to ride in a wagon," Fargo said. "I don't think he's fit to sit a horse."

"Get him out of here," Beale said, and Slater man-aged to get Logan to his feet.

Logan could hardly walk, but he could almost hobble. Slater half dragged him from the scene.

"I'll bet Logan's balls are bigger'n a camel's head," Sergeant Carter said, laughing. "Beggin' your pardon, Miss Gallagher, ma'am."

"That's all right, Sergeant," Sarah said.

She walked over to Fargo, who had holstered his pis-tol and was watching Hi Jolly. The camel driver seemed completely unaware of what had happened. He rolled his prayer rug up and looked around as if to say, "Why is everybody watching me?"

When nobody responded to his unasked question, he walked calmly away without speaking.

After he'd left, the others slowly drifted away, except for Sarah and Beale.

"I can assure you that won't happen again," Beale told Sarah. "And I apologize for the men."

"They should apologize themselves," Fargo said.

"I'll see to it that they do. And thank you for stepping in, Fargo."

"Glad to be of help," Fargo said, and Beale took his leave.

"You didn't have to help me," Sarah said when Beale

was gone. "I can take care of myself. I don't need some man to come to my rescue."

"You didn't need me to get you off that camel, either."

"That's right. I didn't. I'll thank you to mind your own business from now on."

"Now that you mention minding my own business, what were you doing here? Did you have some business to take care of?"

Sarah blushed. "I was following Logan and Slater. I'd seen Hi Jolly come back here, and I was afraid those two were going to do something to them. And they were. I could have taken care of myself, though, without your interference. You can leave things to me from now on."

Fargo thought it would serve her right if he did. He said, "Where's your brother?"

"What does that have to do with anything? Randall isn't my keeper. It's not his job to keep watch on me every second."

"Somebody had better watch out for you," Jane Montgomery said, emerging from behind a rock where she'd apparently been watching the scene while remaining unobserved. "If they don't, you're going to get into serious trouble. Those two troopers are the kind who like to get rough with a woman if you know what I mean. And I think you do."

Sarah didn't seem to welcome Jane's sudden appearance or her comment.

"You should know," she said.

Jane didn't respond except to give Sarah a dazzling smile. Sarah returned it with a smile that was equally bright, but in spite of all the smiling, or more likely because of it, Fargo thought he would have been more comfortable if the two of them had started pulling hair and throwing punches.

"I was just trying to help," Jane said after a few seconds of uncomfortable silence. "I've been around a few soldiers in my time, and most of them are as kind and gentle as anybody else. But some of them think that putting on a uniform gives them the right to be just plain mean. That's how those two are. You should be glad Fargo was around to help."

"I can take care of myself," Sarah said, and she turned and walked away from them, leaving them alone.

"Did you ever hear of a play called *Hamlet*?" Jane asked.

"Shakespeare?" Fargo said.

Jane nodded.

"I've heard of it. That's about all. I don't get a lot of time to read, but I saw it acted out on a stage once. Why?"

"There's something in it about ladies who protest too much. I just wondered if maybe Sarah was like that."

Fargo remembered the line.

"Maybe she is like that. Not my business, though, as she keeps telling me. Not yours, either."

"Just what is your business, Fargo?" Jane said, cutting her eyes up at him from under the brim of her hat.

"I'm just a guide, that's all."

"I think you're more than that. There's something about you that makes you seem different from the other men on this little expedition. I'd like to find out what it is."

"Maybe you'll get a chance to do that," Fargo told her.

She gave him a smile as brilliant as the one she'd given Sarah, but there was an entirely different meaning in it.

"I certainly hope so," she said.

7

The rest of the day went fine. The camels moved steadily along, and at times the wagons had trouble keeping up. Getting the camels down for the evening had proved to be another adventure in caterwauling and complaint, but it had been done without injury to any of the men or camels.

The more he saw of the camels, the more Fargo was amazed at the things they could do. They could snake their long necks just about anywhere, it seemed, and he saw one of them chewing at its tail. How it could have gotten its head around in that position, Fargo had no idea.

He'd seen nothing more of Logan and Slater, and he hoped they had the good sense to stay out of further trouble. He was pretty sure Logan wasn't going to be feeling like doing much of anything for a day or so. And that was just fine with Fargo.

They camped that night near a spring that Fargo knew of, and when they ate that evening, Fargo found himself chewing his beans and bacon next to Franklin Biggle. The firelight reflected redly off Biggle's glasses as the geologist bent to scoop up a spoonful of beans.

The beans were too salty to suit Fargo, but he wasn't going to mention it. He'd learned never to criticize the trail cook. The cook didn't appreciate it, and he was likely to get his revenge by adding something a lot less pleasant than salt to the beans if too many people complained.

Biggle hadn't ridden as many trails as Fargo, and he was less hesitant to express his displeasure.

43

"These beans are too damned salty," he said. His mouth twisted in an expression of distaste as he looked around as if searching for·the cook.

"I'd keep my thoughts on that to myself if I were you," Fargo told him and explained why.

Biggle frowned. "Hell, a man could go a long time without a decent meal under those conditions. You aren't pulling my leg, are you, Fargo?"

Fargo said that he wasn't. "But this is an army cook, so maybe he wouldn't do anything like that. Maybe he's too disciplined."

"I'm not taking any chances," Biggle said. "I won't complain to anybody else."

"You'll get used to the cooking," Fargo said. Then, to change the subject, he asked if Biggle had found anything interesting so far.

"Not a thing. But I've heard stories that say farther out West there are rocks that are red, all red. And not just some of the rocks. All of them. I'm hoping to find out if that's true, or just some trail rider's story."

"It's true," Fargo said. "I've seen it. But we'll be going a little south of there."

Biggle couldn't hide his disappointment.

"We could swing north, couldn't we? It could be the high point of the trip for me."

"We'll see. I thought you might be looking for something more valuable than red rocks."

Biggle laughed and set down his plate.

"Is the coffee any better than the beans?" he asked.

"You'll have to find out for yourself. I haven't tried it yet."

"At least it'll be hot," Biggle said. When he'd filled his tin cup he settled himself back down beside Fargo. "You've heard some stories yourself, I suppose. The ones about gold."

Fargo grinned, a little sheepishly. "I guess we've all heard them."

"You've been to this part of the country before, you said, so you should know better. You can tell just by looking that this isn't mining country."

"What about the Spanish? I've heard stories about Coronado."

"You think they hid some of their gold way out here? I suppose it's possible. Coronado did find his way to that big canyon up north. But I doubt that he had any gold with him. Why haul it all the way out here? If it's hidden anywhere, and I'm not convinced that it is, it's in Texas. Or New Mexico."

Fargo didn't mention the caves that he and Kit Carson had talked about. He finished his beans and bacon. Salty or not, it was the only meal he was going to get, and he wasn't going to waste any of it.

"So there's no chance we'll run across anything valuable like that?"

"Not much of one, not judging from what I've seen so far. What do you know about the Indians a little farther west?"

"The Hopis? Not much. I never had much to do with them."

"Well, I can tell you what I've heard, and that's that they're not exactly the richest people in the world. If there were gold, don't you think they'd know about it?"

Fargo had to admit that it seemed likely.

"So there's no gold, Fargo. That's just some old wives' tale. You can forget about it. I'm just here to record what I see, not to find any gold. We're not going to get even a glimpse of anything like that."

Biggle took a last sip of coffee and got up. He was about to leave when Fargo reminded him to take care of his plate.

"You can scrub the plate with sand or take it to the spring and wash it out," Fargo said.

"What about the beans?"

"You could always try them on the camels."

Biggle laughed and picked up his plate.

"I don't think of myself as a cruel man, Fargo. I'll dispose of them some other way."

"Time might come when you wish you'd eaten them."

"Maybe so," Biggle said. "But not tonight."

Fargo watched him as he walked away. What was it that Jane had said about protesting too much? He wondered if that applied to Biggle as well as to Sarah.

He looked down at his empty plate. Maybe, he

45

thought, it didn't apply to either one, but it was something to think about.

Fargo slept a little apart from the others because that was the way he wanted it. The others had reasons to be associated. Except for Hi Jolly, they were members of the same troop, or the same families, or at least the same party of explorers. Hi Jolly didn't have any of those associations, but he had the camels, and he slept near them.

Fargo was different. He wasn't involved with anyone except himself, a man apart, hired to do a job.

Before he shook out his bedroll, Fargo took a walk around the fringes of the camp. The camels had finally quieted down. Fargo saw a small, strange-looking tent, which he supposed was where Hi Jolly was bedded down.

The black night sky was sprinkled with glittering stars, and the moon was on the wane. It would be a lot darker before morning.

Fargo wasn't worried about the night or what might happen before dawn. He was thinking of the morning, and of a long, dry wash that the expedition was planning to travel through before they'd gone very far. It would be the perfect place for Manuelito to attack them if he planned to do it. Fargo thought he'd better get up early and ride out to do a little scouting before the others got started.

But he saw no signs of the Navajos now, though that didn't mean much. If they were around, they wouldn't be letting anyone know.

Fargo had gotten well outside the circle of the camp when he heard something scrape on the rocky ground not far behind him. He ducked behind a rock and pulled his .45.

He waited quietly. After a couple of seconds he heard another scrape. A dark figure passed in front of him, and he stepped out of his hiding place.

"All right," he said. "You can stop right there."

"That's fine with me," Jane Montgomery said. "I've found what I was looking for." She turned to face Fargo, who holstered his pistol. "Were you going to shoot me?"

"You shouldn't sneak around like that. I thought you might be Slater."

"Not Logan?"

"I don't think he's able to sneak yet."

"I wasn't sneaking," Jane said. "I was following you, but I wasn't sneaking."

"Why were you following me?"

Jane closed the distance between them. Fargo could see her more clearly now, and she was smiling slightly.

"I told you that I wanted to find out about you. I think the best way to do that is to talk to you privately. That hasn't been easy to do."

Fargo looked around.

"This is about as private as it gets," he said.

"I know. It seems that every time I've seen you, Sarah Gallagher has been around. Is there something going on between the two of you?"

"Not a thing," Fargo said.

"You wouldn't mind if there were, though, would you?"

That was true, but Fargo didn't see the need to admit it. "A man doesn't talk about that kind of thing."

"Some men do. I'm glad to know you're not that kind. You see? I've found out something about you already."

"What else did you want to know?"

She stepped even closer to him, so close that they were almost touching. Fargo could feel the heat coming off her, the way it came off a rock that had been in the sun all day.

"Just one thing," she said.

"What's that?"

She pressed herself against him. His rod was already straight and hard, and he knew she could feel it.

"I think I have an answer," she said, and she leaned into him.

Fargo could feel her rigid nipples through the fabric of her shirt and his own buckskin. He imagined he could even feel how hot they were.

She looked up at him, and he bent down to kiss her. Her mouth was a volcano, and their tongues tangled in a brief dance.

Jane pulled away and said, "Now I know even more

47

about you. Is there anywhere around here where we can talk?"

She was breathing fast, almost panting.

"Talk?" Fargo said.

"You know what I mean, damn you. Is there a place?"

Fargo took her hand and led her behind the rock where he'd been concealed. It was dark with shadow, and there was a clear spot on the ground. It wasn't soft, but it would do.

Jane opened her shirt.

"Don't waste time, Fargo."

He didn't. He shucked off his boots and removed his shirt and pants. By the time he was undressed, Jane was ready. She was completely naked and when she pressed against him again there was no question about the heat of her nipples. They were like branding irons, and his shaft was equally hot and hard, resting between them like iron straight from the forge.

After another kiss, Jane pushed Fargo back against the rock, and he felt its rough surface scraping against his back. Jane dropped to her knees. She took his engorged tool in her mouth and teased it with her tongue. Soon it was wet and slick, and she was moving her head expertly, using her tongue judiciously, and driving Fargo just about out of his mind. If she kept it up much longer, he was going to explode.

But Jane knew when to stop. She smiled up at him, then stood.

"Help me on, Fargo," she said. "I'm ready to go for a little ride."

With his back braced against the rock, Fargo reached around her, cupped his hands beneath the firm, smooth cheeks of her buttocks, and lifted. Jane leaned into him and helped him to support her by placing her feet on the rock.

When the tip of his ivory shaft touched the crinkly hair of her nether lips, he lowered her and slipped into her slick tunnel.

The effect on Jane was instantaneous. She braced her feet on the rock and rode Fargo like a skilled jockey. She rose and fell and twisted, panting all the while, her long black braid flailing her back as her head whipped from side to side.

Fargo's own back was rubbed against the rock, tearing the skin, but within seconds he was past worrying about the pain because he was experiencing too much pleasure in other locations.

Jane's nipples burned into Fargo as she rode, and she started to make short, breathless cries.

"Ah. Ah. Ah. Ahhh!"

Suddenly she threw her head forward and bit down on Fargo's shoulder to keep from screaming aloud as a wave of passion rose up her body and crested in her brain. She shuddered like a woman thrust into a snowbank, but she was burning instead of freezing. Fargo shot boiling streams into her, one after another, like the volleys of a cannon.

After it was over, Jane hung limp against Fargo, who was leaning back against the rock, still supporting her with his hands.

"That . . . that was really something, Fargo," Jane said, pausing occasionally to catch her breath. "I don't think I've ever . . . had a ride like that."

Fargo didn't think he had, either. At least he couldn't remember one at the moment. The backs of his legs were weak, as if he'd been completely drained of strength.

But evidently he hadn't.

"What's that I feel, Fargo?" Jane said. "My God, don't tell me that you . . . Yes. You are, aren't you."

Fargo was. He was growing hard inside her, something he wouldn't have thought was possible only seconds before. But there wasn't much question that he was, and before either of them had time to think very much about it, Jane was off for another ride. It was slower this time, the climax less violent.

It took Jane a little longer to get her breathing regulated this time, but when she did, she said, "Now I know what you're good at, Fargo. And why you seem different from the other men. I don't think a one of them could do what you just did."

Fargo wasn't sure he could do it again, himself. He

49

lowered Jane to the ground, and the two of them slowly got dressed.

"I'd better get back to my father now," Jane said. "He'll be worried about me. You take care of yourself, Fargo."

Fargo said that he planned to and watched her walk back toward the camp. He'd intended to complete his circuit of the camp before going to sleep, but he wasn't sure he could make it. He barely had the strength to walk back to his bedroll. He was asleep almost as soon as he lay down.

8

The next morning Fargo was up before dawn. His back was scraped raw, there were tooth marks in his shoulder, and he didn't feel fully rested, but he didn't mind. The escapade with Jane had been worth it. He still felt a little weak in the knees, too, but he was able to sit his horse with no trouble, and he rode away from the camp after letting Sergeant Carter know where he was going.

"You really think those Navajos are gonna come after us?" Carter asked.

"I really do," Fargo said. "Manuelito's not likely to let an insult like the one we gave Short Knife pass without some kind of repayment."

"What d'you mean, *we* gave him? You know damn well it was Logan and Slater. The rest of us didn't have a thing to do with it."

"Manuelito doesn't care who it was. It was a soldier, and that's us, even the ones who aren't wearing a uniform. He's not going to attack the fort, not when there's an easy target wandering around outside the walls. He's out there somewhere, waiting."

"I sure hope you're wrong," Carter said.

"So do I," Fargo told him.

But he didn't think he was.

Fargo rode toward the west with the sun tinging the sky pink behind him. Somewhere back there, Fargo knew, Hi Jolly was saying his morning prayers.

The ground was rough, dry, and stony. It hadn't rained in ages, and it wasn't likely to for a long while. That was just as well, Fargo thought, because a dry wash could become a death trap if there was a sudden hard thunderstorm.

As he rode, he looked for any sign that Manuelito was in the vicinity, though he didn't really expect that the Navajo chief would be careless enough to leave one.

So in the absence of signs, Fargo tried to put himself in the chief's place. If Manuelito was out there waiting, where would he be hiding?

When Fargo got to the wash, he looked along the banks as far as he could see. In the distance there was a place where a few straggly oak trees fronted some high rocks. That was the most likely place for an ambush, and Fargo scanned the area for a way around the wash.

Fargo rode back along the edge away from the trees and eventually found a spot where he thought the expedition could cross the wash and then follow the opposite bank instead of going down into the bed. The bank was going to be a bit rougher than the bottom, which was mostly sand smoothed out by the water that ran through after the occasional rains.

If Beale was right about the camels, they wouldn't have any trouble with the terrain, so Fargo rode back to camp to see if everyone was ready to move out.

When Fargo explained to Lieutenant Beale about his change in plans, Beale agreed readily to the new route.

"You'll see, Fargo. The camels will have no trouble at all. I can't vouch for the horses and wagons, however. Are we likely to break a wagon wheel?"

Fargo wasn't worried about that, and said so.

"The rocks aren't that big, and the ground's level enough."

"Good," Beale said. "Then let's move out."

Fargo rode ahead, and the expedition got started. As Fargo heard the bawling and complaining of the camels, he wasn't sorry he'd been gone when they'd been readied for travel. They would have been in a much worse mood then.

After looking things over and being certain that the way ahead was clear of Manuelito's Navajos, he rode back to see how Jane and her father were doing.

He didn't get to them, however, because Sarah Gallagher stopped him. She seemed completely at ease on Samuel now, having adjusted well to the animal's odd swaying stride.

"I want to ask you something," she said after getting Fargo's attention.

Fargo felt a little uncomfortable riding alongside the camel with Sarah seeming so far above him. He preferred to have people he was talking to more or less on a level with him.

"Ask me, then," he said, looking up at her.

"Have you noticed anything strange about Mr. Montgomery?"

Fargo wondered what she could be talking about. He said he hadn't noticed a thing except that Montgomery seemed a little frail.

"That's what I'm talking about. It's almost as if he's been ill for a long time."

Fargo said that everybody had noticed that.

"Then what I'd like to know is why he came. Isn't this a dangerous trip for an old man?"

"He came because he was available," Fargo said. "The man who was supposed to help Johnson with the surveying was hurt in some kind of accident."

"Oh. Maybe that explains his problems, then."

"What problems would those be?" Fargo wanted to know.

"My brother was talking to him about some of the surveying points. They have to work together because Randall's drawing the maps."

Fargo said he knew that.

"Of course. But Randall says Mr. Montgomery isn't very good at it. He had to go get Clyde Johnson to clarify things for Randall."

"Montgomery's old," Fargo said. "Maybe he was tired."

"I suppose that's it," Sarah said. "Last night I happened to be passing by his wagon. I don't think he saw me. He was looking around for Jane, but he couldn't find her."

Fargo had a pretty good idea why, but he didn't think there was any use in mentioning it.

Sarah looked down at Fargo. "You wouldn't have any

idea where she might have been, would you?" she said in a suspicious tone.

"I was asleep," Fargo said.

"Anyway," Sarah went on, the suspicion still not gone from her voice, "Mr. Montgomery seemed very energetic when he was looking for her."

"This climate's good for a man's health," Fargo said, thinking that he'd been pretty energetic the previous evening, too.

"You could be right," Sarah said. "The air is certainly bracing. Where were you going when I stopped you just now?"

"Nowhere," Fargo said, and after bidding her a good day, he rode back to the head of the column.

They came to the area where Fargo suspected that Manuelito might be hiding without incident, but Fargo had a feeling they were being watched the whole time.

So did Carter. He rode up to join Fargo, who sat on the Ovaro and watched the column move slowly past him.

"You think they're over there behind those rocks?" Carter said.

"Could be," Fargo answered. "If I were Manuelito, that's the place I'd pick."

"And you think they're just gonna sit there and let us go right past 'em without a fight?"

"They might. They'd have to ride through the wash to get to us, and the bank's steep on both sides. We'd have too much of an advantage. We'd kill half of them while they were still down at the bottom. They don't have many good weapons. Lances and arrows aren't much good against men who are firing down at you with rifles."

"They've got some guns," Carter said.

"Not many, from what I've heard, and the ones they have are old, stolen down in Mexico."

"That's pretty much right. And there's another thing we've got in our favor."

"What's that?" Fargo asked.

"Them damn camels."

"What about the camels?"

54

"The Indians ain't never seen 'em. Well, they might've had a look at 'em when they came into camp the first time, but I don't think so. Manuelito was too far away when that happened, and since then they've been inside the crazy corral most of the time, except when Miss Gallager had one out for a ride."

Fargo thought about what Carter had said. It was likely that one of the Indians had sneaked a look inside the corral. He would have been puzzled by what he saw, and he would have reported it to Manuelito, who would have been equally puzzled.

If the Navajos were seeing the camels in action for the first time, they might be confused enough to put off an attack. They might even be a little frightened. Fargo wasn't ashamed to admit that the camels had given him an anxious minute or two when he'd first seen them. Hell, they still did.

"Maybe we don't have anything to worry about then," Fargo said. "But I won't be happy until we're out of Navajo territory."

"I don't blame you," Carter said, "but I think everything's gonna be just fine."

As it turned out, he was mistaken.

There was only about a quarter of a mile left to go along the edge of the wash before it turned to the north and then snaked away for a few miles and finally disappeared, but Fargo wasn't ready to heave any sighs of relief.

The camels hadn't taken to the rocky soil quite as well as Beale had said they would. Maybe the rocks where they came from were bigger, or smaller, or fewer. For whatever reason, the camels didn't like the conditions, and they were letting everyone know about it. The caterwauling had become almost continual, and it was getting on Fargo's nerves.

That might not be so bad, he thought. If it's bothering me, Manuelito must think we're riding some kind of demons.

It was also bothering the troopers and the horses, and that was what caused the trouble. Corporal Vinson's horse strayed too close to the camels, and one chomped down on the mount's neck. The horse whinnied and bucked, jerking away from the camel's toothy grip.

Vinson hauled back on the reins and got the horse turned. He was almost in time, but the horse stepped on a rock, and its right front leg went flying out at an angle. Man and beast tumbled over the side of the wash and slid down to the bottom in a cloud of rocks and dust.

Fargo was the first to the edge. The horse was lying on its side, Vinson trapped beneath.

The man was moving, but the horse wasn't.

Carter rode up beside Fargo. "Who's gonna go down there after him?"

"It'll take more than one of us," Fargo said. "We'll have to get the horse off him."

He looked down the side of the wash. It was steep and rocky and treacherous.

"We could just ride down to the end of the wash," Carter said. "Take us a little longer to get to him that way, but it'll be a sight easier."

Beale had joined them by that time and he blamed himself for the accident.

"I should have warned everyone about the bad temper of the camels. They can sometimes strike out at whoever's closest by them."

"We all knew about that," Carter said. "Vinson should've been more careful."

"I'll get some men to go down and help Vinson," Beale said. "Who would you suggest, Fargo?"

"Carter and I will go. We could use some help. How about Rollins and Taylor?"

"I'll tell them," Beale said and whirled his horse around.

Carter looked back down the wash to the rocks and the oak trees.

"What about them Navajos?" he said. "You reckon they're still there?"

"I think we're about to find out," Fargo told him.

9

They rode into the wash and reached Vinson as quickly as they could, leading an extra horse.

Vinson was alive but unconscious, moaning faintly. His right leg was trapped under his dead mount, and Fargo figured that his leg was broken.

The sun beat down. All the men were hot, but Vinson's uniform was soaked through with sweat.

"We better get that horse off him and get him out of here," Carter said. "Fargo, you and Rollins and Taylor lift up on the horse, and I'll drag Vinson out from under it."

Rollins was a short, bandy-legged man with shoulders as wide as a doorway. Fargo thought he ought to be able to lift the horse by himself, and he was glad he'd come along.

Taylor was the opposite of Rollins—slat-thin, tall, and wiry. He might not be strong, but Fargo didn't think he'd let them down.

The three of them hunkered down and got the best grips they could. Fargo had hold of the front of the saddle, and Rollins had the back. Taylor had the neck to himself.

Carter slipped his hands into Vinson's armpits and said, "Heave to it."

The three men strained to lift the dead animal. Fargo hoped to hell the cinch girth didn't break.

It didn't. The men's boot heels slid and scrabbled for a hold. When they found one, the men exerted all their strength, sweating and straining until they were able to raise the horse just enough for Carter to slide Vinson out.

As soon as Vinson was clear, Fargo and the others let go, and the horse fell back down.

Vinson didn't look good. His face was doughy white and there was blood on his uniform near the knee of his broken leg. A large knot swelled on his forehead.

"He's hurt so bad a little more won't make any difference," Carter said. "Put him on the horse, Rollins."

Rollins picked Vinson up as if the trooper weighed no more than a sack of grain, but Rollins was too short to heave him over the back of the extra horse. Taylor went to help, and that was when Fargo heard the Navajos.

No one had been watching for the Indians, who'd been forgotten for the moment. The men at the bottom of the wash were busy with Vinson, and the people at the top were watching the ones below trying to rescue him.

Manuelito had taken that opportunity to attack. Fargo turned and saw the Indians riding hard down the bank of the wash opposite the caravan. There was no cover for them—they were willing to risk themselves for the chance to get the unprepared men who were saving Vinson.

An arrow whizzed by Fargo, and another struck Taylor in the neck, going straight through. Blood spurted, and Taylor fell backward. Rollins staggered under the sudden shifting of weight, but he managed to sling Vinson across the back of the horse.

Fargo heard gunshots, and a couple of puffs of dust danced up nearby. More arrows fell around them, and a lance smacked into Vinson's already dead horse.

The troopers opened fire on the Navajos, and several fell from their mounts.

"There's nothin' we can do for Taylor," Carter said. "Let's get the hell out of here."

Fargo glanced down at Taylor. The arrow had severed one of the big arteries in his neck. The ground beside him was stained darkly with blood, and the pool was still growing. If Taylor was alive, he would certainly be dead by the time they got out of the wash.

But Fargo couldn't just leave him there. He bent over, took hold of Taylor's belt, and hoisted him up. He got his arms around his body and flung the man over his saddle.

Fargo didn't take the time to tie Taylor on the horse. He pulled himself up on the Ovaro. Rollins was already well on the way out of the wash, leading the horse that held Vinson, and Carter was right on his heels. Fargo followed, pulling the reins of Taylor's horse, which galloped along beside him.

About a dozen of the Indians had ridden ahead of the others to cut off the exit from the wash. Fargo recognized one of them as Short Knife, and he was in the lead.

Fargo dug his heels into the Ovaro's side, and the big horse surged forward.

"Keep going!" Fargo yelled at Carter and Rollins. "I'll try to stop Short Knife."

Fargo hoped he'd have a little help from the troops, but he couldn't count on it. He pulled back on the reins to slow the Ovaro. Then he drew his .45 from the holster and fired at the Indians.

Hitting a man from aboard a running horse wasn't easy. In fact it was downright impossible, but Fargo got lucky on the first shot, and he knew it. The bullet took Short Knife right in the brisket. The Navajo threw up his arms, gave a loud cry, and fell sideways off his horse, hitting the ground in a cloud of dust.

The other Navajos appeared surprised and shocked at what had happened to Short Knife, but they must have been even more shocked to see what was heading in their direction.

Hi Jolly was leading troopers on camels in a race toward the exit of the wash, and seeing that many camels on a dead run was enough to shock anybody, including Fargo, who for a few seconds forgot all about the Indians while he watched the camels run.

Hi Jolly seemed completely comfortable on his wobbly perch, like a man in a rocking chair on his front porch. He had a rifle, which he fired into the midst of the Indians, who were frozen in place as they watched the big beasts that ran toward them.

It was only a matter of time before someone's nerve broke, and when one of the Indians turned his horse and fled, the others followed him without hesitation.

The camels rumbled after them, and to Fargo they no longer seemed awkward but somehow as fluid as racehorses.

Now that the danger was past, Fargo got off the Ovaro and tied Taylor onto his horse, not that it mattered much. The trooper was dead.

Fargo made sure he did the job right and remounted. He nudged the Ovaro with his heels and soon enough he'd caught up with Carter and Rollins.

They left the wash, turned toward the caravan, and saw that the firing was still going on across the wash. But the Navajos were hopelessly outgunned, and they were taking heavy casualties. They were able to get a few arrows across the wash, and a couple of troopers were down, but the Indians were suffering far more.

Then the Navajos saw the others coming back in their direction, pursued by strange animals that ran like nothing they had ever seen before.

Manuelito wasn't stupid. He knew when to cut his losses, and he called a retreat. The Navajos turned their horses and headed back in the direction they'd come from.

The troopers didn't follow, but they'd done enough to convince Fargo that camels could run at least as fast as horses when called on to do so. He might even think about riding one himself someday.

"You've stepped in it now," Carter said to Fargo as they watched the Indians go, pursued by the cavalry on camels.

"How's that?" Fargo asked.

"Hell, you killed Short Knife. He's what this whole thing was about, and now he's dead. You don't think Manuelito's just gonna go home and sit in his hogan and forget about it, do you?"

Fargo knew that was too much to hope for, but he didn't want to talk about it.

"What about Short Knife's body? You just gonna leave it there?"

"Manuelito will come back for it."

"Yeah, but by then the buzzards will have been at it. We oughta do something about that."

"First let's get Vinson to Tolliver and see what he can do for him," Fargo said.

"I want you to know I appreciate what you tried to do for Taylor," Carter said.

"Don't mention it," Fargo said.

"Compound fracture of the tibia and fibula," Tolliver said, pushing up his helmet. "Shinbones to you. Not so good."

Tolliver had thick black hair and dark blue eyes set in a swarthy face that made the blue color of his eyes even more startling, though they were usually hidden in the shade of his sola topee.

Even Fargo could tell it wasn't good. The bones protruded through the skin where Vinson's uniform had been cut away from his leg. It was too bad that Vinson had regained consciousness because the pain must have been awful. Carter had done what he could, giving Vinson a bottle of whiskey and ordering him to drink it.

"The whole damn bottle," Carter said. "I don't care if you think it'll kill you. It won't come as close to doin' the job as that leg will."

"Where'd you get the whiskey?" Fargo said. "I didn't think it was allowed."

"Never you mind that," Carter said. "You can see we needed it. What about that leg, doc?"

"We'll just have to do what we can," Tolliver said.

"And what the hell might that be?"

"First we'll have to try to get the bones aligned. Drink some more of that whiskey, soldier. This is going to hurt."

Vinson looked for just a second as if he might be going to cry. But he didn't. Instead he took a long pull at the whiskey bottle.

"It would be best if we had something to tie the ends of the bone together," Tolliver said. "But since we don't, we'll just have to make do with a splint. First, though, we need to sterilize the break. I have some medical alcohol."

He gave Carter a look. Carter ignored him.

61

"I'll go get it now," Tolliver said.

He went away, and Vinson continued to drink. Fargo felt sorry for the man, more of a kid really. He was never going to walk normally again, not with the leg being fixed out here where there was no bed to rest in and no time to rest even if there had been one.

Tolliver came back carrying a bottle of clear liquid and a stick. He unstoppered the bottle and squatted over Vinson's leg.

"This is going to hurt," he said. "Bite on this stick."

He took the whiskey from Vinson and handed the bottle to Carter. Then he put the stick in Vinson's mouth.

"Bite now," he said. "Hard."

And when Vinson bit, Tolliver poured the alcohol directly on the wound.

Vinson twitched like a man with Saint Vitus's dance and nearly bit the stick in two, but he didn't pass out, and the stick held together. It might have been better if Vinson had fainted, Fargo thought, because what came next was even worse.

"Keep biting that stick," Tolliver said. "We're going to straighten that leg of yours."

To do that and to get the bones aligned, Rollins held Vinson's shoulders and Fargo held his waist, while Tolliver pulled the leg straight and more or less got the ends of the bones together.

This time, Vinson did pass out. Fargo didn't blame him a damned bit.

Tolliver made splints of a board that Carter got from one of the wagons and tied them on the bandaged leg with strips of cloth.

"That's the best I can do," Tolliver said when it was all over. "He should be in a hospital to give the ends of the bones a better chance to knit together, but there's no chance of getting to one. We could send him back to the fort in a wagon, though."

Lieutenant Beale said that was out of the question.

"Manuelito would never let a wagon get through," he said, and Fargo knew he was right. "Vinson will have to stay with us."

"If he does there's a good chance that the leg won't heal properly, or that gangrene will set in," Tolliver said.

"Then it's a chance we'll have to take," Beale told him. "It's a certainty he'll die if we try to send him back, and whoever goes with him will die as well. He stays with us."

"I can't be responsible for him."

"Nobody said you had to. I'm the leader of this expedition, and I'll take the responsibility."

"Very well," Tolliver said.

"I'm glad you agree. Now let's get Vinson in a wagon and get out of here."

10

"What do you think, Fargo?" Carter asked. "Can an Indian pony find its way home?"

Fargo was sure that it could, but he wasn't sure tying Short Knife's body to the horse and letting it roam away was the best thing to do.

"If it don't get home, that might not be a bad thing," Carter said. "Havin' your body carried around by your horse, is I'm sayin'. Beats bein' buried to my way of thinkin'."

Fargo said he wasn't sure Manuelito would agree. "And the horse might not like it, either. Not after a while."

"Body'd tend to get pretty ripe, all right. Well, what do you think we should do, then?"

The two of them had stayed behind to take care of Short Knife's body when the column moved out. Beale had given them permission after Fargo had assured him that the next few miles of the journey wouldn't present any hazards.

"We'll put a blanket over him," Fargo said. "And a few rocks. Just enough to keep the buzzards off."

"Rocks, huh? I don't guess you ever thought of missin' him."

"I didn't think I'd hit him, much less kill him. It was a lucky shot."

They finished the job and caught up with the expedition by midafternoon. There were no further problems from either the camels or the Navajos for the rest of the day, but Fargo was certain that Carter was right and that they hadn't seen the last of Manuelito. He was sure to try to get even for the death of his cousin. Fargo didn't know just what form the vengeance would take. He supposed he'd just have to wait and see.

They camped that night at a spring where the water flowed out of the ground in a number of places, but where the various streams never came together to make a large pool. Instead it ran all over the low ground and created something akin to a marsh, with small pools scattered around it.

"I sure thought we'd be goin' through more of a desert," Carter said to Fargo that evening. "This sure don't look like a desert to me."

"Deserts can have more than sand and cactus," Fargo said. "Some of them have rocks."

They were standing a good distance from where Hi Jolly was overseeing the unburdening of the camels for the night, but the sounds of their bawling carried for quite a distance in the cool evening air. Fargo was beginning to get used to it.

"I heard this country was a sand desert, though," Carter said.

"Farther south, it is. Here, it's mostly rocks and hard ground. And there's even springwater. We'll see some mountains and canyons before we're finished, too, but not a lot of sand."

"Guess that's fine with me. I like all this water. Sure beats doin' without."

Although the water had collected into a number of small pools, none of them was large enough to jump into for a bath. But many of them were plenty big enough to provide ample water for the people, horses, and camels, though the camels didn't really need much.

"How's Vinson?" Fargo asked.

"He's doin' about as well as you'd expect. I think he has some fever, but they're keepin' him still and lettin' him have a little whiskey."

"He needs to eat."

"That's what Tolliver said, but it might be a while before he feels like it."

Carter looked to the west, where the sun was going down behind a long line of black cloud. The rim of the cloud was outlined with pink and orange. Fargo admired it for a while and then turned back to the east.

"You think Manuelito is out there somewhere?" Carter said. "Somewhere close, I mean."

Fargo was sure of it. He said, "But we won't know how close until he wants us to know."

"Just him, you reckon, or his whole bunch?"

"Most likely it's just him," Fargo said. "He wouldn't bring the whole tribe. He saw me shoot his cousin, and he got a good look at me. So I'm the one he has the quarrel with."

"You get a good look at him?"

"I've seen him before."

"You seen that scar on his chest?"

Fargo said that he had.

"How'd he get that?"

"Shot with a Spanish musket," Fargo said. "Or so I heard. Anybody that can survive something like that's bound to be one tough Roman."

"Maybe he won't come after you," Carter said.

"He'll come," Fargo said. "But like I said, we won't know when he gets ready for me until he wants us to."

"Maybe he'll get tired of followin' us."

Fargo laughed. "Don't count on it," he said. "Let's go thank Hi Jolly for leading the charge this afternoon."

When they got to the camels, most of the work had been done. The mercurial Hi Jolly was looking on and correcting the men in his own style if they didn't do things to his satisfaction.

"May the fleas of a thousand camels infest your pubic hair," he told one hapless trooper who was trying unsuccessfully to get an unloaded camel to stand up and move away. "You know nothing of how to handle these fine animals. Where are the men who came to Fort Defiance with Hi Jolly? They knew about camels. They are the ones who should be here now."

"Some of us are here," Private Spence said. "And if you want to know the truth, we'd just as soon be somewhere else."

"You do your job correctly," Hi Jolly said. He pointed out another trooper. "Now help this poor son of goat do his, or we will be here all night."

Spence moved to help, and Fargo took the opportunity to tell Hi Jolly that he appreciated his leading the charge earlier in the day.

"It was my pleasure to do it. We have showed the American savages how real warfare is made, riding on these noble beasts. I believe that they could not have escaped us had Lieutenant Beale not called us back. The Navajos will not soon return to test the wrath of Hi Jolly."

"Your 'noble beasts' are what caused the trouble in the first damn place," Carter said. "If one of 'em hadn't bit Vinson's horse, we'd be a sight better off right now than we are. And Vinson wouldn't be half dead."

Hi Jolly ignored him. "We will not be bothered again. You will see."

"I can't talk to a fella like you," Carter said. "Come on, Fargo. Let's get some supper."

Later that night Fargo went on another scouting excursion around the camp. He was surprised to come upon Jane Montgomery and her father in close conversation in the shelter of a cottonwood tree on the edge of the marshy area. They didn't see Fargo, who remained in the shadows of some other trees. Though he couldn't hear what they were saying, he sensed anger between them. Soon enough, however, they leaned close together, and the older man put his arm around his daughter's shoulders with what seemed to Fargo more than fatherly affection.

Fargo had hoped he might have another visit from Jane that night, but now he figured he was going to be disappointed. She and her father seemed too wrapped up in their conversation to leave any room for him.

He skirted well around them and circled the perimeter of the camp, ranging out into the marsh. He could see fires flickering in front of some of the tents behind him, but no one seemed to be moving around. Then he heard splashing in a pool not too far away.

He pulled out his .45 and moved in the direction of the noise. He thought it might be some animal, as it wasn't likely that Manuelito would be so careless as to let anyone hear him.

It wasn't Manuelito, and it wasn't an animal. It was Sarah Gallagher, who had slipped away from the camp to bathe in the cool, clean water.

The pool was wide, but it was too shallow for her to get into it. So she had removed her clothing to crouch down by the water and splash it on her before washing off with a cloth that she had in one hand.

Fargo holstered his pistol and stood watching. There wasn't enough moonlight for him to see very well, but what he could see was worthy of admiration.

She knelt so that he could see her in profile. Her blond hair was unbound, and fell around her face. Her breasts stood out proudly, the nipples taut from the cold. Fargo considered their pleasing shape and the round curve of her hips.

After a short while she picked up another cloth and stood up to dry herself.

Fargo stepped closer and said, "Good evening, Miss Gallagher."

She turned, covering herself as best she could with the cloth she'd been drying with. She didn't seem surprised to see him.

"I was wondering if you were going to say anything, or just sneak away," she said, looking him in the eye.

"You knew I was here?"

"I know you have a high opinion of yourself, Fargo, but you aren't the only one with a keen eye and ear. You made as much noise as one of the camels. Or maybe it was just the heavy breathing."

"It wasn't that," Fargo said.

"Then why do you keep looking at me that way?"

Fargo wasn't aware that he'd been looking at her in any particular way, and he said so.

Sarah stood up a bit straighter and held the cloth more tightly against her.

"Ha. You're just like every other man. You think women would like nothing better than for you to force your attentions on them. Well, I'm not like that, Fargo. Maybe somebody on this expedition is, but it's not me."

"I don't know what you're talking about."

"Jane Montgomery has been making calves' eyes at you since she first saw you. And don't tell me you haven't noticed."

Fargo could have told her that Jane had been doing a lot more than casting longing looks in his direction. "What if she has?"

"If she has, it's only because she wants something

68

from you. You might think it's because you're dashing and handsome, but that's not it, Fargo. A woman like her always has some other reason."

"Are you saying you think I'm dashing and handsome?"

"I most certainly am not."

Fargo heard the sound of a boot rasp across the rocky soil a second before Sarah did. Her eyes widened, and Fargo turned, drawing his pistol.

"Sis?" Randall Gallagher said. "Are you out here?"

Sarah screamed. Not loud enough to be heard in camp but loud enough for Randall to hear her. Fargo turned back to her and saw the towel drop to the ground. It was a pleasant enough sight, but Fargo was afraid that the consequences weren't going to be pleasant at all.

"Sis?" Randall said again, and blundered into sight.

Fargo returned his pistol to its holster, knowing it didn't look good for him to be standing there with a naked woman and trying to figure out why Sarah had dropped the towel.

"My God," Randall said, looking at the two of them. His fingers curled into fists. "Fargo, you worthless bastard!"

Fargo didn't have time to respond—Randall charged toward him, his head down like a bull, his arms swinging wildly.

Fargo just had time to brace himself before Randall barreled into him, carrying him backward for several feet. Their feet churned the water for a few steps, and then they both toppled into the pool with a splash that sent water into the air cascading all around them.

Fargo knew the water wasn't deep, but it was deep enough to cover his face, and that meant it was deep enough to drown in if someone held him under it. And that was exactly what Randall was doing.

Randall had wrapped his long arms around Fargo, trapping Fargo's own arms at his sides. They had landed in the pool with Randall on top, and as far as Fargo could tell, he had no intention of moving off.

Fargo struggled to get his head above the surface of the pool. Randall butted him in the forehead.

Sparks danced behind Fargo's eyes, and he fell back under the water. He was still conscious, and he'd been able to take a shallow breath after Randall butted him. But he didn't know how long he could hold it.

He could dimly hear someone, it had to be Sarah, yelling at Randall, but Randall wasn't paying any attention and wasn't distracted. He tightened his grip on Fargo, squeezing out what little air Fargo had kept in his lungs.

Fargo felt a deep burning in his chest, as if a fire had been lit there, and he knew he'd have to take a breath in seconds. His fingers scratched at the bottom of the pool for something, anything, that he could use as a weapon. He felt slimy moss, thin mud. Nothing that would help.

Just as he thought his lungs would burst open inside his chest, the fingers of his left hand closed on a rock. He couldn't hit Randall in the head with it, not with his arms pinned, but one end of it was jagged and sharp. Fargo brought it up as far as he could. Unable to strike with any force, he stuck the jagged end of the rock into Randall's back, then gouged and twisted as hard as he could.

It was just painful enough to surprise Randall into loosening his grip. When he did, Fargo's head popped out of the water, and Fargo took a deep, gasping breath.

Then he went back under.

Randall must have been puzzled as to why Fargo didn't keep his head above water because he looked down to see Fargo's face.

When he'd gotten as close as Fargo thought he was going to, the Trailsman swung his head up and butted him in the nose.

Butting had worked for Randall, to a certain extent, and it worked even better for Fargo, who felt rather than heard Randall's nose break.

Randall gave a strangled cry and let go of Fargo. He fell over into the pool, and Fargo shoved him aside. Then he stood up with water dripping off his buckskins as he sucked in more air.

The next thing Fargo knew, Sarah was pounding him with her fists. She hit him in the face and chest before he could grab her wrists and hold her off. She was still naked and slippery as a catfish, but Fargo didn't let go, even when she started kicking him. Her feet were bare and not doing any damage.

"What the hell is the matter with you?" he said.

"You tried to kill my brother!"

"I think you have us mixed up," Fargo said. "Your brother was trying to kill me."

He shoved her away from him, and she fell backward, splashing down hard in the pool beside Randall, who was sitting there holding his nose and moaning.

Fargo walked over and picked up the towel that Sarah had dropped. He threw it to her and told her to cover up.

"And get dressed," he added.

She glared at him, but she started to dry off. Fargo waded over to Randall.

Kneeling down beside the mapmaker, Fargo said, "I don't know what you thought was going on here, Gallagher, but whatever you thought was wrong. I was just out having a look around the camp and came on your sister."

"You sub of a bidtch."

"You need to have Tolliver look at that nose. He can pack it and tape it, and that'll help a little. I'm afraid it'll never be quite as straight as it was before, though."

"Sub of a bidtch."

Fargo stood up and took hold of Randall's arm. He jerked the other man out of the water and up to his feet. Randall kept one hand over his nose, which was bleeding just a little. The blood ran down past the corner of his mouth.

"Your sister should be about dressed by now," Fargo told him. "She'll help you get back to the camp and find Tolliver. He'll fix you up."

"Sub of a bidtch."

"I know you're hurt, Gallagher, but if you say that again, I'm going to tear what's left of your nose right off your face," Fargo said.

"You wouldn't dare," Sarah said from right behind him.

"Don't try me," Fargo said.

He walked away and left them there.

11

The next week passed quietly. Fargo saw little of Sarah Gallagher and her brother, and when he did, they did their best to ignore him. Randall's nose was healing nicely. Tolliver had done a good job.

What Fargo still hadn't figured out was just exactly what had happened that night at the marsh. He knew that sooner or later he was going to have to talk to both the Gallaghers and see if they could set him straight. But they weren't ready for that yet, and he wasn't sure he was, either.

Sarah would be the first one he'd confront. She was the one who'd dropped her covering and caused her brother to become so furious that he'd tried to kill Fargo. At least Randall had sense enough not to try anything further. Maybe Sarah had explained things to him. That was what Fargo hoped to find out.

News had a way of getting around quickly in a small group of people who were traveling together, and everyone had heard some version or other of what had happened in the marsh. Sergeant Carter had ribbed Fargo about the fight but hadn't pried into the causes of it too deeply. Fargo knew why. Everyone suspected that the fight had been about Sarah, and since it was a delicate subject, no one was going to come right out and ask Randall or Sarah what had happened.

Lieutenant Beale had called Fargo aside and asked about it, and Fargo had assured him it was all a misunderstanding. Beale had accepted the explanation without going too far into matters that might prove indelicate, and Fargo didn't think anyone else would question him directly.

But he was wrong. One day at noon Jane Montgomery sought him out and sat down beside him while he was eating.

"That Gallagher cow tried to get you killed, didn't she," Jane said after talking for a few minutes about inconsequential matters.

"I don't much think we should talk about that," Fargo said.

Jane ignored his comment.

"You know why she did it, of course."

Fargo put down his plate. The cornbread had been hard, and the beans had been about half cooked. He'd eaten most of it, but he couldn't quite finish.

"I don't know what you're talking about," he said.

Jane dismissed his denial with a wave of her hand.

"Sure you know, Fargo. You're not an idiot."

Fargo didn't think he was an idiot, and he'd had plenty of experience with women. That, however, didn't mean he understood them. In fact, no matter how many women he knew, he'd never quite understand them. And he had a feeling that was the way they wanted it.

"Maybe I am an idiot," he said. "You'll have to explain it to me."

Jane sighed. "Sarah Gallagher is one of those women who wants people to think she's entirely self-sufficient. She can ride a camel as well as any man can do it. She can do this, she can do that. But deep down, she's scared of something. She wants her brother to be there and take care of her. I'm sure that was all he was trying to do when you beat him half to death."

"I didn't beat him half to death. I hardly touched him."

"You broke his nose. That's close enough to a beating for me. And I'll bet little sister arranged the whole thing."

When he thought about it, Fargo had to admit that Jane had a point. Sarah had dropped the towel, deliberately making things look much worse than they were to encourage Randall to protect her. And big brother had charged ahead without thinking to ask anyone what the real circumstances of the situation might be.

"He's short," Jane said. "She makes him feel big. And he makes her feel protected. You have to admit it's a cozy arrangement."

It sounded all too likely to Fargo, but he still planned to have that conversation with Sarah as soon as she stopped avoiding him. He'd let her tell him her side of it before he made up his mind.

In the meantime, Fargo was uncomfortable talking to Jane about it. He said, "What about your father? How's he doing?"

"He's fine. He might look old, but he's tough."

From what Fargo had heard, that was true enough. Montgomery was proving much more durable than anyone had thought he would. But he wasn't proving to be much of a surveyor. Fargo didn't care. That wasn't his problem.

"And what about you?"

"I'm doing very well, as you can see. I enjoyed our little . . . visit the other night. Maybe we can do it again."

Fargo thought that was a fine idea. "When?"

"We'll just have to wait and see about that. But for now, you watch out for Sarah Gallagher. She'll get you in more trouble if you're not careful."

Fargo said he'd do his best, and Jane got up and left. She'd given Fargo plenty to think about.

Slater and Logan had also been avoiding Fargo, and they had as good a reason as Gallagher. But they hadn't been avoiding Hi Jolly, and Fargo thought that was going to lead to more trouble.

Lieutenant Beale had told them to stay away from the camel driver, and they had, when Beale was around. But Fargo had heard from Carter that they'd done a number of things that Beale wasn't aware of.

"Sneaky little bastards," Carter said when he caught up with Fargo after eating. "Nobody ever catches 'em at it, but I know it's them. The Lieutenant does, too, but he can't do anything about it until somebody sees 'em in the act."

Fargo asked what they'd done.

"There was a scorpion in Hi Jolly's blankets one night."

Fargo laughed. "I've seen a scorpion or two this last week, myself. One was in my boot this morning."

"Yeah, and I've seen a few of 'em, too. But Hi Jolly says this one was put there."

"He can't be sure of that."

"That's what you say. As for Hi Jolly, he's pretty damn sure it was put there, and he's mighty mad about it. And what's worse, somebody pissed on those prayer rugs of his."

"How does he know that?"

"Hell, Fargo, he can smell it. So could I when he brought 'em to me to complain. They're rank as a skunk's ass. To tell you the truth, I don't think it was Logan or Slater's piss. Too gamy. I think they took 'em and let the camels piss on 'em."

"Beale should do something about those two," Fargo said.

"He would if he could. Like I told you, they're sneaky. I thought maybe you and me could kinda keep a watch on 'em, see if we can catch 'em doin' anything."

"I'll keep my eyes peeled."

"You got 'em peeled for anybody else?"

"You mean Manuelito?"

"That's who I mean, all right. It's been a week or so now, and we ain't seen hide nor hair of 'im. You reckon he's give it up and gone home?"

"Since we've never seen him, maybe he never followed us."

"Humpf. You know better'n that. He was out there for a while. I could feel 'im, and you could, too. Now . . . well, I'm not so sure."

Fargo told the sergeant that he was sure. He hadn't seen any signs, but he knew Manuelito was out there. Like Carter, he could feel him.

"What's he waitin' for, then? Looks like he'd have made his move by now."

Fargo didn't know what Manuelito was waiting for, any more than Carter did. Maybe a time, maybe a place. Maybe just the right opportunity. But whatever it was, he was out there. Fargo couldn't have explained how he knew that, but he knew it just the same.

"Well," Carter said, "all I can tell you is, you'd better watch your back and be careful."

"Seems like everybody's telling me to be careful today," Fargo said.

"How's that?"

"Never mind," Fargo said. "I'm going to check on Vinson. Want to see how he's doing?"

"I'll just be movin' along. I already spoke to him today. He's a good young fella, and he's gonna be fine."

Fargo hoped Carter was right about that. That broken leg hadn't looked good.

The trooper was lying in the back of Tolliver's wagon, and in fact he did seem to be doing fairly well. He'd had fever for several days after the accident, but now his face was no longer flushed, and he'd started eating a little better.

"If you and those other men hadn't come after me," he told Fargo, "I'd be full of Navajo arrows right now."

"You can thank Hi Jolly, too," Fargo reminded him.

"I've done that. He's a fine fella. A little funny in his ways, but still a fine fella."

"Not everybody feels that way," Fargo said.

"That's what I hear. If I find out who it is, they'll have to answer to me."

Fargo smiled. Vinson had sand, but it was going to be a good while before he was going to be able to make anybody answer to him.

"I know what you're thinking," Vinson said, "but I'll be up from here before you know it."

"I'm betting you will," Fargo said. "But you can leave whoever's bothering Hi Jolly up to me. I'll see that they're taken care of."

"I'd appreciate it if you could do that. Hi Jolly did right by me, which is more than I can say for some folks."

"Which folks would those be?" Fargo asked.

"You know who I'm talking about."

Fargo shook his head, pretending ignorance, though he had a pretty good idea. But he wanted to hear Vinson say it.

"Slater and Logan, that's who. Those two have been

trouble ever since they joined up with us at Fort Defiance."

"What kind of trouble?"

"You saw that horse race, so-called. That's not the first time something like that's happened."

Fargo thought more people would have known about it if Slater and Logan had cheated at the races before, yet nobody had mentioned it. He asked Vinson why.

"I'm not talking about the races, but I think they've cheated in those, too, now that you mention it. Anyway, what I'm talking about are card games and a crooked dice game or two."

Dicing and card playing were the ways soldiers often whiled away their time, and Fargo wasn't surprised to hear Vinson's suspicions. Men who'd cheat in a race might cheat in other things.

"Are you sure they cheated?" he asked.

"Hell, yes. I wouldn't say a thing like that about a man if I wasn't sure of it. Oh, not everybody agrees with me. They can't see how it was possible. But those two are slick. They put it over real smooth, and if you weren't watching close enough, you'd miss it."

"You were watching, though," Fargo said.

"I sure was. After they skinned me once, I decided I'd do a lot more watching and a lot less betting. I never caught 'em at it, not with any evidence I could use in a court or anything, but I know they were switching out the dice and bottom dealing in the card games. I called them on it once, but they denied it, and somehow the dice had got changed back to the ones they started out with."

Fargo wondered if Vinson was telling the truth or just trying to excuse his own bad luck and poor gambling skills.

"I don't think they've had any games of chance on this trip," he said.

"They won't bring out the cards or the dice where the Lieutenant can catch them. But you wait till we get to Fort Yuma. They'll be playing again there."

Fargo wouldn't be joining in. He didn't intend to be gambling with the likes of Slater and Logan because he didn't play cards with men he didn't trust unless he had a good reason.

"I think they'd gambled a lot of other places before they ever got in the army," Vinson said. "They played well enough to have fooled a lot of folks before they fooled me."

"I'll stay out of any games with them," Fargo said. "I don't think they'd invite me, anyway."

Vinson grinned. "You sure gave that Logan something to think about. I wish I'd seen it. He was walking around like he was real tender for a couple of days. He any better yet?"

"He's okay," Fargo said. "But he was hurting for a while there, I think."

"I think so, too," Vinson said, still grinning. "And you know, there's somebody else I'm wondering about."

"Who's that?"

"I'd better not say. It's nothing I'm sure of, and I don't like to start stories going around. Before long, everybody believes them, whether they're true or not. I'll let you know if I can find out if I'm right."

"You do that," Fargo said.

He shook hands with Vinson and left him there. The trooper's grip was firm, and Fargo knew he was going to be just fine.

But five days later, he was dead.

12

"I just don't understand it," Tolliver said. "I thought he'd be up and walking before we got to California. His bones were knitting better than I ever expected, he was eating and drinking, he was clear of fever. I just don't know what happened."

"Gangrene?" Carter asked.

"Not a sign of it. No infection at all. He was doing as well as if we'd sent him to the best hospital in the East."

Vinson had died during the night. Sarah Gallagher, who had taken to visiting him every morning before mounting up on her camel, found him in the back of the wagon.

"He looked as if he died in pain," she said. "Why didn't he cry out?"

"He must not have been able to. Private Temple was sleeping nearby. He would have heard him."

"Temple could sleep through a thunderstorm," Sergeant Carter said.

"Not through a cry of pain," Tolliver said. "No one sleeps through that."

"Could something have happened during the night?" Sarah asked.

"Something could always happen," Tolliver said. "Maybe something connected to the leg. An embolism, possibly. But nothing should have happened. He was fine, just fine."

Fargo thought Vinson's death had hit Tolliver harder than anybody, probably because Vinson had been doing so much better than the doctor had expected.

"You can't save every patient," Jane Montgomery

79

said by way of comfort, but her words didn't seem to affect Tolliver.

Fargo had to give Jane credit for trying to help. She'd been a regular visitor to Vinson while he was recovering.

"I never saved anybody," Tolliver said. "I trained to be a doctor, but I found out soon enough that I wasn't really suited to the work. That's when I turned to botany."

They were all standing not far from the spot where Vinson had been buried only a few minutes earlier. Digging in the hard, rocky soil had been difficult and slow, so it was now close to midmorning.

"Was there anything strange about the body?" Fargo asked. "Any marks or wounds?"

"No," Tolliver said. "Other than the broken leg, Vinson seemed to be in good health."

"That's not what I mean," Fargo said.

"You're suggesting that he might have been killed?"

"That's right."

"Why would anybody want to do that?"

"I'm not sure. But if somebody did, I want to find out."

"We all want to find out," Carter said. "Vinson was a good man and a good soldier."

"There wasn't anything that would suggest he was killed," Tolliver said. "I almost wish there had been. The back of his heel was scraped, as if he kicked his good leg in his death throes, but that was all. I wish I could have done more for him."

"You don't have to blame yourself," Jane said. "You did all you possibly could."

Tolliver shook his head. "You're right, but it wasn't enough."

Up until Vinson's death, the expedition had gone smoothly. Maybe too smoothly, Fargo thought. Their good luck had to run out sooner or later.

Some little things had gone wrong, the way they always did on any expedition: a broken wagon wheel, a lame horse, a thrown mule shoe or two, a few mild cases of dysentery, a couple of fistfights among the troopers. Those sorts of things were to be expected. But no one had expected someone to die because of an accident.

There was no minister among the people on the expedition, so Beale had conducted the funeral. He'd read from the Bible and said a few words over the grave. Even Hi Jolly had seemed to listen, which caused Carter to say that maybe the camel driver wasn't as much a heathen as he'd first thought.

"One thing's for sure," Carter told Tolliver now. "There's not another thing you can do for him."

On that happy remark, the little group separated. Fargo caught up with Sarah Gallagher before she managed to get back to her brother, who was discussing something with Clyde Johnson and waving a paper at him.

"I'd like to talk to you," Fargo told Sarah.

She turned and looked at him, her blue eyes flashing. "And why should I let you do that?"

"Because you owe it to me. You nearly got me killed, and I want to find out why."

Sarah looked toward her brother, who was still engaged in his conversation with Johnson, and Fargo took hold of her arm and turned her away.

"You don't need your brother to protect you from me. I'm not going to make any assault on your honor. Come to think of it, I didn't do that the last time, either."

He led her to a secluded spot on the other side of one of the wagons.

"Randall's right about you," Sarah told him when they were sure they were in a private place. "You are a bastard."

"Randall's going to get his nose broken again if he doesn't watch his mouth," Fargo said. "As for you . . ."

"As for me, what? Are you going to break my nose, too?"

"No, I wouldn't do that. But I might have to turn you over my knee and tan your hide."

"You wouldn't dare touch me."

Fargo gave her a smile.

"You might be surprised at what I'd dare."

"You can't talk to me like that. I'm not like that Jane Montgomery."

"She seems like a fine woman to me," Fargo said,

thinking about Jane and the way her braid had whipped the air when she had mounted him. The only thing he could find wrong with her was that they hadn't repeated that encounter.

"Naturally you'd say that. I know how men feel about a woman who isn't any better than she has to be."

"What about a woman who shows herself to a man and then tries to get him killed. What do you call her?"

Sarah looked shocked. "You surely can't believe that I showed myself to you on purpose."

"That towel you dropped wasn't heavy," Fargo said. "You wouldn't have dropped it if you hadn't wanted your brother to think something was going on between us. You teased me and then you stirred up a fight."

Sarah flung up her arm to slap him, but she was too slow. Fargo grabbed her wrist.

"We won't be having any of that," he said.

"Bastard!"

She tore her arm from his grasp and ran around the wagon, disappearing from his sight.

Fargo sighed. He had a feeling she was going after Randall, which would mean Randall would come looking for Fargo, which would mean there'd be another fight, which would mean that Randall would get his nose broken again, if not something even worse.

Fargo stayed where he was. If there was going to be a fight, he wanted it to be as private as possible. No need for everybody in the camp to see it.

It didn't take long for a red-faced Randall to show up. He came around the end of the wagon at a lope. His nose was still red, and it was going to be slightly off-center for the rest of his life. He stopped short when he saw Fargo.

"You've been bothering my sister again," he said, which Fargo thought was a promising beginning. Randall was angry, and his fists were balled, but at least he had begun the proceedings by talking instead of by bulling into Fargo headfirst.

"I wasn't bothering her," Fargo said. "I just wanted to talk to her."

Randall took a deep breath and let it out slowly.

"I don't want you to talk to her."

"When you came on us the other night," Fargo said, "nothing was going on. I don't know what you think you saw, or what Sarah told you later, but I just happened to walk up on her while she was bathing. That's all there was to it."

Randall drew himself up a little straighter and stared at Fargo for a long moment. He said, "I don't think a gentleman should even be discussing the situation I found you in."

"I never claimed to be a gentleman," Fargo said. "But we need to get this cleared up between us, and we can't do that without talking about it. You have the wrong idea about me. What did your sister tell you?"

"I didn't discuss it with her."

"Because you're a gentleman."

"That. And other things."

Fargo was curious about the other things, so he asked about them.

"It's really none of your business," Randall said. "It's something that shouldn't be discussed outside the family."

Fargo was getting a little tired of Randall Gallagher. He had so strict a code of honorable behavior that Fargo wondered if there was anyone left in the world for him to talk to except his sister.

But instead of getting angry, Fargo thought maybe he could appeal to Randall's sense of honor.

"I think it *is* my business, Gallagher. You tried to drown me in that marsh, and you damned near did it. I'd think I have a right to know why. I think I deserve a straight answer."

Randall opened and closed his fists, breathing heavily through his half-open mouth.

"I've told you why," he said.

"You haven't told me anything. I'm the one who's done all the talking. I told you that nothing happened between your sister and me, but all you do is say there are things you can't talk about. I think you can tell me about them. You just don't want to."

For a while Randall didn't speak. He stood there looking at Fargo and taking deep breaths. Fargo didn't know what Randall was thinking about, but gradually some of the red color began to leave his face and his breathing sounded more normal.

"I've been having some problems lately," Randall said. "A lot is going wrong. Maybe I was just taking some of my anger out on you."

"What's been going wrong?" Fargo asked.

Randall shook his head. "It's Montgomery. He knows very little about surveying. Johnson is fine, and we're getting the maps made, but it's not as easy as it should be."

"I saw you talking to Johnson a while ago. You were showing him a paper."

"We were discussing some of the latest mistakes. Johnson will get them straightened out, I know, and I shouldn't let that interfere with my judgment. If I've wronged you, I apologize."

"I appreciate that, and I'm sorry I broke your nose. Now, do you want to tell me about your sister?"

"No," Randall said. "But I suppose I will. Maybe I do owe it to you."

Fargo waited, but Randall said nothing more for a full minute. Then he seemed to get himself under control.

"It's something that happened years ago," Randall said. "It was my fault, and I still feel guilty about it. Sarah's never gotten over it, and she's never forgiven me."

"If it happened years ago, maybe it's time she did both."

"It's not the kind of thing you forget," Randall said. "And I don't blame her for not forgiving me. It's the worst sort of thing that can happen to a woman."

Fargo had been given enough hints. He thought he knew the subject that Randall was trying to avoid.

"Was Sarah raped?" he said.

Randall's shoulders slumped. "Yes. Our parents are dead, and I've taken care of Sarah since she was just a girl. One day we were out riding. We weren't far from home, and we thought there was no one around but us. Then two men came out of the trees along the trail. They had guns, and they made us stop and get off our horses. They tied me up, and they raped Sarah. She's never gotten over it. And neither have I."

84

Randall turned away after telling his story as if he couldn't bear to look Fargo in the eye, though Fargo couldn't see what Randall had to be ashamed of.

"The men had guns, and you didn't," Fargo said. "What could you have done?"

"I could have done *something*. But I didn't. I let them tie me up, and then I had to listen while they attacked my sister. It was . . . pretty bad."

Fargo felt sorry for the Gallaghers, not just because of what had happened but because of the way it had changed their lives. Jane had been right about Sarah, who now felt that she had to be as good as a man at anything she tried, and she never stopped wanting to prove herself.

At the same time, she wanted her brother to be there if something went wrong, the way it had when she was raped. And she was halfway afraid of men, probably all men. She was both attracted to them and scared by them. She didn't mind leading them on, but she wasn't going to let them do to her what the rapists had done, even though she must have known that it wouldn't be the same.

"Please," Randall said. "Don't let Sarah know I told you any of this."

"I won't," Fargo promised.

"And stay away from her," Randall said. "I mean it, Fargo."

"Whatever you say," Fargo told him.

13

It took only the rest of the day for the rumor to spread that Hi Jolly had killed Vinson.

Fargo didn't know how it had started, though he figured he had a pretty good idea. It was Carter who told him about it.

"They're sayin' he was killed for his poke," Carter said. "I don't know that he had much money, but if he had any, it was missing from the wagon."

"What does the Lieutenant think of all this?" Fargo asked.

"About what you'd think if you were in his position. He's worried that it's going to cause more trouble, and he's worried that somebody might try to do something to Hi Jolly."

Fargo remembered something that Carter had said back before their journey had even begun.

"You told me once that Hi Jolly might murder us in our sleep so he could take our money and buy things with it."

"Dammit, Fargo, you remember too much. I know I said that, but it's different now. Hi Jolly is a damn good man. You saw how he led the charge against Manuelito when we pulled Vinson out of that wash. I was wrong about him, and I don't mind admittin' it."

"Where is he now?"

It was late afternoon, and the expedition had stopped for the night. They hadn't covered as much ground that day because of their late start, but Fargo didn't think it would be a good idea to try traveling after dark.

Carter looked up at the sky, which was going slate

gray except in the west where the sunset colored it fiery reddish gold in a wide line that stretched all along the horizon.

"It's time for his prayers," Carter said. "You think we oughta see how he's doin'?"

"It might not be a bad idea," Fargo said.

They found Hi Jolly kneeling and praying, his back to the sunset. If he was worried about anything, Fargo couldn't tell.

Carter and Fargo waited until Hi Jolly had finished his ritual before they approached. When he had rolled up his rugs, Fargo walked over and said, "You heard what they're saying about you?"

Hi Jolly looked disdainful.

"I have heard. May the crawling lice of the desert infest their crotches and feast on their testicles."

Fargo grinned. It didn't sound like a bad idea, as long as it wasn't directed at him.

"This is serious, Hi Jolly," Carter said. "Somebody might kill you in *your* sleep if you don't watch out."

"Hi Jolly did not take the dead man's money, no matter what anyone might say. In the countries where I have traveled, a man's hand is removed if he steals. I like my hands, and I am not a thief."

"I know you're not," Carter said. "So does the lieutenant, and so does Fargo. Ain't that right, Fargo?"

Fargo said it was, and Carter went on. "But somebody here don't like you, and that's why that story got started. The question is, who started it?"

"You should know the answer to that," Hi Jolly said. "Even a camel, no, even one of your mules should know."

Carter turned to Fargo. "He's talking about that damn Slater and Logan, ain't he?"

"That's who I'd put my money on," Fargo said. "Those two have been troublemakers from the start. Where did they come from, anyway?"

"Now that's the funny thing," Carter said. "Don't nobody seem to know. 'Course nobody asks, either. If a man don't want to talk about that kind of thing, nobody's gonna push him on it."

There were people who joined the army because they wanted excitement or adventure or just a steady job, Fargo thought, and there were people who joined to get away from something. Fargo had a feeling Slater and Logan might fit into the latter category.

"We won't be able to prove they started it," Carter said. "They're too damn sneaky for that."

"We'll just have to make sure nobody believes them," Fargo said.

Carter nodded. "Yeah. But that won't be easy."

"I'll talk to Lieutenant Beale."

"You do that," Carter said.

The best plan that Beale and Fargo could come up with was for Beale to assemble everyone after supper and address them about the rumor.

He called it a low and scurrilous slander, and he mentioned Hi Jolly's actions on the day Vinson had been hurt.

"Nobody who helped save a man's life would kill him later," Beale said.

The lieutenant stood straight and serious by the cook fire, and the shadows danced around him. He made an impressive figure, Fargo thought, but the Trailsman wasn't sure if Beale was convincing anybody, least of all Slater and Logan, both of whom looked bored. Slater was scraping under his fingernails with the point of a bowie knife, and Logan was leaning back against a wagon wheel with his eyes half closed.

"Dr. Tolliver has told us that Private Vinson died of natural causes," Beale continued. "His broken leg no doubt contributed, even though we aren't sure just how. There was no sign of foul play, and I don't want to hear any more of these offensive lies about Hi Jolly. He's essential to our expedition, and I expect you to treat him with civility."

When Beale had concluded, Fargo could hear a few men muttering about Hi Jolly's heathen ways, but others shut them up by reminding them that Hi Jolly had more than held up his end of things.

The funny thing was that the more Fargo heard about

Vinson not having been killed, the more likely it seemed to Fargo that he had been.

Vinson had been coming along fine. He looked better every time Fargo saw him, not at all like a man who was in any danger of dying.

Even if there wasn't any evidence that Vinson had been killed, Fargo was bothered by the fact that the back of his heel had been scratched. If Vinson had experienced some kind of rigor or fit, why wasn't there more evidence of it? Fargo thought there was more to Vinson's death than they'd discovered so far, and he thought it might be a good idea to keep an eye on Hi Jolly that evening.

And he would have if he hadn't been distracted by Sarah Gallagher.

She came up to him after Beale had finished and said, "Would you mind walking with me?"

"I promised your brother I'd stay away from you," Fargo told her.

"I don't care what you told Randall. He and I have talked things over, and he's agreed that I should speak with you. Now will you walk with me or not?"

"It would be my pleasure," Fargo said.

He couldn't help noticing that Jane Montgomery was watching them. She had a smirk on her face, and she gave Fargo a slight nod, as if to say, "I know what she's up to."

Sarah took Fargo's arm, and they walked out beyond the circle of the campfire and past the wagons, but not out of sight of the camp.

Sarah made a comment about the brilliance of the stars and then got right to the point.

"Randall shouldn't have told you what he did. He had no right."

"It explained why he acted the way he did," Fargo said. "It made me feel a little better about him."

"It didn't make me feel any better," Sarah said. "The thought of what happened makes me feel dirty."

"It was a long time ago. And nothing that happened was your fault."

"I know that, but that doesn't make it any better. Did he tell you who the men were?"

89

"That's something he didn't mention," Fargo said, and it had never occurred to him to ask. He'd assumed that Randall didn't know.

"They were friends. People we knew. They'd known us since before our parents died. They comforted us afterward. We believed in them."

Fargo thought that explained even more about Sarah and Randall now, especially Sarah. No wonder she found it hard to trust anyone.

"What happened to them?"

"They went right back to their respectable lives. I suppose they're still living in that town. I have no way of knowing."

"You mean you ran away?"

Sarah gave him a defiant look. "We didn't run. We went to the sheriff first, and then to the judge. Neither one of them believed us. They said that the men were fine, upstanding citizens and that we were just a couple of hysterical youngsters."

"You should have gone to a preacher."

"One of them *was* a preacher."

Sarah walked a little distance away from Fargo. He let her go. The more he heard of the story, the worse it got.

Sarah turned around and came back to where Fargo was waiting. She said, "Randall was always good at mathematics, and we had an uncle who made maps. We moved near him, and Randall studied with him. I studied, too. When it comes to mapmaking, I'm not as good as Randall, but I'm not bad. I can ride and shoot and do a lot of things as well as any man."

"Maybe you should try doing a few things as well as a woman."

Sarah tensed, then slowly relaxed. "I suppose I deserved that. I . . . I've tried to be a woman. I think I was trying with you at the marsh. But the more I thought about it, the more frightened I became. And when I heard Randall, all I wanted was for him to fight you."

"Well, you got your wish."

"I had two wishes. I got the second one."

"What if he'd killed me?"

"Then I'd have been terribly sorry," Sarah said. "I know I was wrong. But I couldn't help what I did."

"Could you help it now?"

"What do you mean?"

"I mean that we could make something happen about that first wish."

Fargo reached out and took hold of her arms. For a second or two she yielded, but then she went rigid. He pulled her to him anyway and put his arms around her.

She trembled like a panicked bird, ready to fly away at the first opportunity. She tried to lean her head on his shoulder, but she couldn't quite bring herself to do it. She pulled her head back and looked up at his face.

"It won't work, Fargo," she said. "I wish it would—I really do—but it won't."

"You have to give it a chance," he said. "I'm not those two men who came riding out of the trees. They're way behind you now."

She struggled in his embrace, but he didn't release her.

"I know you're not them," she said. "But I'm afraid of what might happen."

"Why are you afraid?"

"Because I like you. Because I'm attracted to you."

"Then you shouldn't be afraid. Just let it happen."

"You don't understand. I want it to happen. I really do. But at the same time, I don't want it to happen. I want it, but I'm afraid of it. It's like I'm being torn apart inside."

"At least you're not calling for your brother."

"No," Sarah said, "but something makes me want to. It's all I can do to keep from screaming."

"You didn't scream at the marsh. You didn't even seem afraid."

"No, of course not. I knew Randall would come to check on me. He'd already told me he would, so I was expecting him. It was just a matter of time until he arrived."

"What if he hadn't come?" Fargo asked.

"I had a pistol with my clothing. I might very well have shot you."

"You don't have a pistol now," Fargo said, running his hands gently over her clothing.

Sarah shivered. "No. I don't have a pistol now."

She seemed to be relaxing gradually, and Fargo was all too aware of her firm body pressing against him. He was aroused, and he knew that in a short time it would become obvious to Sarah that he was. He should let her go, he thought, but he couldn't quite bring himself to do it.

"I know what you want, Fargo," she said. "The same thing all men do."

She'd said something similar before, and Fargo hadn't really thought much about it. Now that he knew what she meant, and why, he felt guilty. So he opened his arms.

"You'd better go find your brother," he said.

14

"I want to leave you," Sarah said. She leaned into Fargo. "But at the same time, I don't. It's time I got over my stupid fears. I rode Samuel, didn't I?"

"You did," Fargo said, who still thought that Samuel was a strange name for a camel. "You rode almost as well as Hi Jolly."

"I know better than that. But I was afraid of Samuel to begin with, until I got to know him. When I learned how to handle him, I was fine."

Fargo didn't like the way the conversation was going. He didn't want to be "handled," made to do Sarah's bidding like a camel, not even if it meant helping her get over her fear of men.

At the same time, he liked the way he was feeling. His stiffened tool was pressed between Sarah and himself, and he knew she could feel it now.

"Is there somewhere we could go?" Sarah said.

Fargo might as well take the risk. If she got frightened and screamed, it wouldn't be any worse than when she'd dropped her towel. He took her hand and led her off into the night.

Before long they came to a couple of big sandstone rocks that stuck up enough to conceal them. Fargo went around them, and Sarah followed.

Fargo wasn't too sure they should be there, what with Manuelito lurking somewhere out in the darkness. In fact, Fargo had wondered more than once if Manuelito might not have sneaked into the camp and killed Vinson.

The Navajo would be silent and deadly enough to do it if he set his mind to it, and it made sense in an odd kind of way. He might indirectly have blamed Vinson for the death of Short Knife, and he could have decided to kill the people he believed responsible one by one.

But Manuelito would have been more direct, Fargo thought. He wouldn't have killed Vinson in a way that couldn't be detected. He would have slit his throat or bashed his head in. Whoever had killed him, if indeed someone had done that, hadn't wanted to be found out.

Fargo hadn't seen hide nor hair of Manuelito, and neither had anyone else. Carter had been looking as hard as Fargo, and maybe even harder, without result. So wherever Manuelito was, he seemed to be keeping his distance from the expedition.

"Are we safe here?" Sarah said, echoing Fargo's own thoughts.

"I think so. But we can go back to the camp if that's what you want to do."

"It's what I should do. I'm not sure it's what I want. You'll have to go very slowly with me, Fargo."

That was what Fargo intended to do. He pulled her to him and held her. She was stiff as a stick at first, but after a while she began to soften against him. He tilted up her chin and looked down at her. She closed her eyes, and Fargo lowered his lips to hers.

When they first kissed, Fargo thought Sarah would break and run, but his arms were around her again, and he held her in place. They broke off the kiss, and Fargo said, "It's better when you help."

"I'm sure it is." She was trembling but made no attempt to move away from him. "Don't rush me, Fargo. I'm trying."

"I won't rush you," he said, and he kissed her again.

This time she relaxed, and her lips parted slightly. Fargo parted them a bit more with his tongue, and her own tongue touched his in response.

And it was as if Sarah had been galvanized. She opened her mouth and inhaled his tongue, pushing herself against him so that he could feel her engorged breasts and the stiff nipples pressing through his buckskin shirt. He held her tightly and returned the kiss until she broke away, panting.

94

"My God, Fargo," she said. "I've never felt this way. I don't want to run. Kiss me again."

He did, and her mouth devoured him greedily. He raised a hand to caress her breasts through the heavy fabric of her shirt, and her nipples stiffened even more. She reached up her own hand to press his harder against her and ground her pelvis against his erect shaft.

When she broke away this time, her hair was disheveled and there was a wild look in her eyes. She unbuttoned her shirt.

Fargo started to tell her that she might want to think things over, but then he realized that thinking might be just exactly what Sarah didn't need to do. There were times when thinking things over was necessary, and even required, but it was thinking and worrying that had gotten Sarah messed up in the first place. Maybe it was time for her to let her instincts take over.

Fargo removed his own clothing. When she came against him, he could feel the whole womanly length of her, all softness and curves, except for the hot, stiff nipples and the crisp pubic hair at the joining of her legs.

After another kiss, she reached down to touch Fargo's thick rod, tentatively at first. When she saw that it wasn't going to hurt her, she took a firmer grip.

"How does that feel?" she said and began to rub it lightly.

"Fine, just fine," Fargo said.

He slid his own hand down until it came to the mound at the base of her stomach. His fingers tangled in the crinkly hair and then one of them slipped quickly between her legs. As the finger passed over her swollen clitoris, Sarah gave a low moan. Her eyes rolled back in her head, and Fargo thought she might faint.

"My God," she said, her eyes still closed. "Do that again, Fargo. But slowly."

Fargo knew what she wanted, and he let his finger slide back and forth in her slit, touching her very softly, hardly even touching her at all. Her breath came faster, and Fargo moved his finger faster. As he did, her hips moved with him, and in just moments, Sarah threw her arms around him and held to him as if she thought she would fly off into the sky if she didn't have an anchor. Her body spasmed again and again, and she pressed her face into Fargo's chest to change her cries of passion into a series of muffled groans.

"Mmmmmmmpf. Mmmmmmmpf. Mmmmmmmpf."

When it was over, she collapsed against him. She would have fallen if Fargo hadn't held her up.

For quite a while, she hung limp in his arms and said nothing. Fargo didn't see any need to talk, either. His rod was trapped between them, pointing straight up.

Finally Sarah looked up. She said, "I want more, Fargo."

She took his hand and led him to a spot where there was a thin covering of grass. She let go of his hand and sat down. Then she lay back and said, "Help me, Fargo."

Her legs spread, and Fargo knelt between them. He leaned over and kissed her breasts, letting his fingers work between her legs for a while until she was slick as a honey pot. Soon she was writhing beneath his touch, and he knew she was almost ready for another explosion.

His shaft felt as if it was about to burst and spill its seed on the ground, so he put the tip of it just within her. She was so wet and ready and frictionless that he slipped in the rest of the way without conscious effort.

Sarah bucked under him, and he didn't know if it was from panic or pleasure, so he paused for a moment. She moaned and moved under him, and when he thrust himself into her again, she matched him stroke for stroke with hips that churned and twisted and brought him to a peak in seconds. He tried to hold back but realized it would be impossible. He streamed into her, and as soon as he did, Sarah experienced an orgasm that shook her from head to toe, drawing even more of Fargo's fluids out. With each spurt, Sarah climaxed again. If Manuelito had appeared with an axe or a knife, Fargo would have been helpless against him.

Luckily no such thing happened, and eventually they lay spent beside each other on the grass, looking up at the spangle of stars overhead.

Sarah broke the silence. "I'm glad I didn't run away, Fargo. I never knew what I was missing."

"I'm just glad that Randall didn't slip up on us," Fargo said.

Sarah hit him in the shoulder with her fist, but she was laughing.

"I'm glad, too," she said. "But I'd better get dressed and get back to the camp before he gets worried and starts looking for me."

Sarah stood up, and put down her hand. Fargo took it and stood as well.

"I want to thank you, Fargo," she said. "For helping me not to be afraid."

"It was my pleasure," Fargo said, and meant it.

They gathered their clothing and got dressed. Sarah said that she'd better go back to camp by herself, so as not to cause too much talk, and Fargo agreed. He wanted to have a look around, anyway.

Sarah kissed him on the cheek. "I won't be afraid again, thanks to you."

Fargo reckoned she'd be afraid again, but she had a confidence now that went beyond her ability to ride a camel or shoot a gun, and Fargo figured that was a good thing.

"You can't let Randall know what happened between us," she said.

"It's not something Randall would want to talk about," Fargo said with a smile. "And I'm not the kind to tell my private business."

Sarah smiled in return and walked back toward the camp. Fargo watched her go, and when he was sure she was safely to the wagons, he started making a wide circle around them to see what he could find.

He found nothing but rocks and brush and the night breeze, and he wondered if he was wrong about Manuelito. Maybe the Navajo didn't have revenge on his mind at all and was back with his people, having forgotten all about the death of his cousin. Such a thing was possible, Fargo thought, but not likely.

He went back to the camp where he saw Clyde Johnson and Frank Montgomery sitting by the wagon that held the surveying equipment. They were drinking coffee and talking. It appeared that they might be arguing, and

Fargo walked over. He stopped short of the firelight to listen.

"I'm getting the hang of it again," Montgomery said. "It's been a while since I did any survey work, but in my day I could run a survey line and figure latitudes and longitudes as well as the next man."

"Maybe you could," Johnson said. His usually cheerful face was twisted in a frown. "But you haven't been doing very well on this expedition. Gallagher's worried about the accuracy of his maps, and so am I. The government's depending on us."

"The government doesn't have to worry about me. I'll hold up my end, but I'm not responsible for Gallagher. Maybe he should spend less time worrying about his sister and more time on his mapmaking."

In the light of the small fire, Montgomery looked old, but his voice was firm and young. And angry.

Johnson stood and spilled the remains of his coffee on the ground.

"Gallagher knows his business," Johnson said. "I just hope you know yours."

Fargo was about to step in, but he was distracted by yelling from the direction of the camels. It sounded as if Hi Jolly might be in trouble, so Fargo left Montgomery and Johnson to their discussion and went to see what was going on with Hi Jolly.

When he arrived at the place where the camels were bedded down, he saw Hi Jolly standing in a small circle of six troopers. His knife was in his hand, and the light of combat was in his eyes.

"Let the man who thinks he can harm Hadji Ali take the first step forward," the camel driver said. "And he will be the first to feel the sting of my knife."

The camels were behind Hi Jolly, and they seemed hardly disturbed by the commotion. They chewed their cuds and farted and moaned. Their smells were as foul as ever in Fargo's nostrils.

"What's going on?" Fargo said.

One of the troopers turned his head in Fargo's direction and said, "We just wanted to ask him what went with Vinson's money. He don't want to tell us."

"You don't even know that Vinson had any money," Fargo said.

"Yeah? Well, who asked you to butt in, anyway?"

"You ain't an officer," said another. "You got no authority over us."

That thought gave them some backbone, and three of them ran at Fargo. The other three went for for Hi Jolly.

Fargo didn't have time to see what Hi Jolly did, as he had plenty of trouble to deal with on his own.

The first trooper reached Fargo in a shambling run, flailing wildly with his fists. He was big and awkward, so the Trailsman stuck out his foot and tripped him. The man fell heavily and skidded forward on his face. He didn't seem likely to get up for a while, so Fargo ignored him in favor of the other two, who were working as a team. One of them came at him high and the other came low and bent over in a crouch.

Fargo kicked the crouched one in the side of the head, and he tumbled sideways to the ground and rolled over a couple of times. The other man managed to get in a glancing blow that grazed the side of Fargo's head, but Fargo hit him with a short, hard blow right under his breastbone, and he collapsed to his knees, gasping for breath.

The man Fargo had tripped was up on his hands and knees, shaking his head as if trying to clear it. Fargo turned to him and kicked him in the stomach. He bent double, then fell flat on the ground. He lay there and didn't move.

The third man was lying still and groaning. He didn't appear to be much of a threat, so Fargo turned back to Hi Jolly, who was standing his ground and swinging his wickedly curved knife from side to side as if it were a miniature scythe and he was the grim reaper.

A trooper jumped toward him, and Hi Jolly slashed at him so fast that Fargo would have sworn he heard the blade of the knife whistle through the air.

The trooper jumped back. Fargo saw that his blouse had been sliced neatly apart, and a thin line of blood crossed his chest.

"Come to Hadji Ali," Hi Jolly said, beckoning to the

troopers with his left hand. "He is but a lowly camel driver. You have nothing to fear."

"They have me to fear," Lieutenant Beale said as he strode up. "What do you men think you're doing?"

The three soldiers who were still on their feet turned at the sound of his voice. The one Hi Jolly had cut held his blouse together with one hand. A camel farted loudly and befouled the air as if commenting on the situation.

"We were just talking to Hi Jolly, sir," one of the men said.

"I can see that." Beale looked around at the men who had attacked Fargo. "And what about these three?"

"They were having a discussion with the scout, sir."

"It must have gotten rather heated. Is that right, Mr. Fargo?"

"You could say that," Fargo told him.

"Very well. All of you men get back to your quarters. Some of you may have to help the ones who were having the discussion with Mr. Fargo."

The three troopers moved away from Hi Jolly and helped the others get to their feet. Two of them were still wobbly and had to be half carried away. The third could walk on his own, but he couldn't seem to keep in a straight line, and his companions had to touch his arm occasionally to keep him going in the right direction.

"There are times when I'd rather deal with camels than with men," Beale said as he watched them go. "I'm sorry about this, Hi Jolly."

The camel driver wiped the blade of his knife on his robes and thrust it back into its scabbard. He said, "They are the ones who would have been sorry, had you not saved them."

"It won't happen again," Beale said. "I promise you that."

He walked away and left them there.

Hi Jolly gave Fargo a speculative look. "How would you like to ride a camel?" he said.

15

The plan for the next day was to cross the Little Colorado River at the mouth of Canyon Diablo.

The canyon itself was almost impassable, even on foot, much less with horses, mules, wagons, and camels. It was a formidable obstacle to anyone traveling west from Fort Defiance and might have proved discouraging to someone who had never been in the area. It seemed almost endless. But Fargo, having traveled that country before, knew that at the river the canyon ceased to exist, and the crossing would be relatively easy.

At breakfast, Biggle insisted that they make camp once they had crossed the river so that he would have time to go into the canyon and make a brief study of the rock strata.

"There's a canyon up to the north of us that makes this one look small," Fargo told him. He took a bite of his fried bread and chewed it. Then he said, "It's too far out of the way for us to see it, though."

"Then I wish you hadn't told me about it," Biggle said. He took off his glasses and polished them on the tail of his shirt. "However, the Diablo will do just fine if I have time enough to look it over."

"We'll be there by late afternoon. Ask Lieutenant Beale if you can have a whole day."

Biggle was sure that he would, as the expedition was supposed to explore the country. He said he was looking forward to seeing the canyon, and Fargo went off to talk to Hi Jolly about riding a camel.

Fargo had no real desire to get on the back of one of the big animals, much less ride one, but Hi Jolly had insisted. He told Fargo that because Fargo had done him a great favor by standing with him against the men who wanted to hurt him, he wanted to do Fargo a favor in return. And the best thing he could think of was to teach him to ride a camel.

Fargo knew that the river bottom they'd be entering shortly was a wide, rolling valley, mostly grassland, with no place for Manuelito or anyone else to hide in ambush. So if Fargo was ever going to learn to ride a camel, this would probably be the best place.

The camels were kept apart from the horses and mules, which like Fargo, hadn't gotten used to their smell. In fact, the mules pretty much refused to go near them.

When he got to the camels, Fargo saw that Hi Jolly was being assisted in the loading by the six troopers who'd attacked him the previous evening. Evidently Lieutenant Beale's idea of punishment was to put the men to working with the cantankerous, belching, and farting animals.

Since there was a better than good chance that one or more of the men would be either bitten or stepped on or both, Fargo thought the punishment was appropriate.

"You don't have your usual crew," Fargo said to Hi Jolly.

"No, and these miserable men are almost worse than useless at the work." Hi Jolly said. "But they will learn, and they will suffer. It is well." He smiled. "Now, let us see to your camel ride."

Fargo followed him to a kneeling camel that looked suspiciously like Samuel, but then all camels looked alike to Fargo.

"Be gentle with him, Fargo," said Sarah Gallagher, and Fargo turned to see her standing behind him.

Her eyes were laughing this morning, and she seemed happier than Fargo remembered having ever seen her.

"I'll do my best," he said. "I'm pretty good at that."

Sarah laughed and looked at Hi Jolly, who seemed oblivious to their conversation.

"As I well know," she said. "I told Hi Jolly I'd be happy for you to ride Samuel. He's the most cooperative of all the camels."

"Then he's the one I want," Fargo said.

"Did you observe when Miss Gallagher rode?" he said.

"I was watching," Fargo told him.

"I did not ask about watching. I asked about observing. Many watch. All too few observe."

"I do," Fargo said.

"Perhaps. Well, as the camel is already kneeling, you do not need to worry about that part. All you need do is mount and ride."

Hi Jolly handed the rope to Fargo, who remembered how Sarah had pulled the camel's head all the way to its side.

Fargo took the rope, and the camel eyed him with suspicion. As soon as Fargo started to pull, the camel's right hind leg shot out and would have kicked Fargo's feet from under him if the Trailsman hadn't been alert.

"I don't think he likes me," Fargo said.

"Camels have little affection for anyone," Hi Jolly told him.

"They can stretch their back legs to reach just about anywhere," Sarah said. "I saw one scratch his hump with a back leg once."

Fargo wasn't interested in the camel's circuslike abilities. He just wanted to get on its back in one piece. So he took a firm grip on the rope and pulled its head around to its side.

"Excellent," said Hi Jolly. "Now be careful, as this . . ."

". . . is the most dangerous part," Fargo finished. "I remember."

Keeping the camel's head pressed into its side, Fargo mounted the saddle and gripped the camel tightly with his knees. When he was comfortable, he loosened the rope little by little until the camel was looking forward again, and with a series of moans and one great fart, the animal started to rise.

It swayed from side to side as if trying to throw its burden off, first to the right and then to the left, but Fargo kept a secure hold with his knees and remained fixed in the saddle. He noticed that the camel didn't smell any better from where he was seated than it had when he was on the ground.

"Now let him walk," Hi Jolly said.

Fargo kept his knees tight against the camel's hide as the big beast lurched forward. He felt a tinge of something like nausea at the first few strides, but he quickly got used to the rocking motion. He knew it would take a long time for him to get comfortable in the strange saddle, longer than he intended to spend there.

After he had let the camel walk for about a hundred yards, Fargo pulled on the rope and forced it to turn around. With its stomach rumbling beneath him, the camel walked back to Hi Jolly and Sarah. Hi Jolly congratulated Fargo on his ride, and Sarah applauded.

Fargo pitched the rope to Hi Jolly, who grabbed it and cleared his throat. The camel folded its legs reluctantly, and when it was kneeling, Fargo stepped off. His legs felt a bit wobbly for a couple of steps, but he concealed that fact from Hi Jolly and Sarah.

"Very good," Hi Jolly said. "Very good for a first ride. You will get better."

Fargo doubted it very much. He didn't intend to get up on the camel again. It had been interesting, but one ride was enough.

"It's time for us to move out," Fargo said. "I think I'll ride my horse and leave the camel for Miss Gallagher."

"Thank you," Sarah said. "I'm used to him, and I think he likes me."

Hi Jolly looked at Fargo and shook his head.

"Camels like no one," Hi Jolly said.

The day's travel was easy and uneventful, and the expedition reached the Little Colorado River a few hours before sundown. The mouth of the canyon was marked by several sandstone buttes about thirty or forty feet high, and they made it hard to miss. They looked very red in the afternoon sun. Biggle was delighted with them and wanted to go exploring up the canyon immediately, but Beale said it would be better to wait for the next day. He did say that Biggle could have a look at the buttes if he wanted to, which mollified the geologist.

He started to get his gear together, and Beale said that it would be all right for him to look at the buttes alone but that Fargo had better go with him into the canyon. Fargo agreed that it would be a good idea.

"Fargo knows the country," Beale said. "And you might need him for protection. I'll send Sergeant Carter along as well."

Randall Gallagher wanted to go, too, but he said that he'd have to spend most of the next day working on his maps, thanks to certain surveying errors. Clyde Johnson looked a little sheepish, but Montgomery was nowhere around, and neither was his daughter. Fargo thought he'd seen her talking to Slater at one time during the day, which bothered him even though he knew it was really none of his business. Jane was friendly with several of the men, including Johnson. Fargo suspected she was being extra nice to the surveyor so that he would overlook her father's ineptitude.

Tolliver said he needed to go along to have a look at the plant life in the canyon.

"We want a complete record of anything unusual that we run across," he said.

When it was settled about who would be going and who would be staying, Fargo suggested that they ford the river before sundown as there was plenty of time.

"And you might want to send out a few men for game," he added. "There are antelope and deer all around here."

They'd been eating plenty of beans and dried meat and bacon, but fresh meat would be welcome.

They crossed the Little Colorado about a quarter of a mile above the spot where a tributary veered off into Canyon Diablo. The crossing was easy enough, as the river was shallow. There was a gentle slope down to the water instead of a steep bank, and though the water ran fast, the bottom was smooth and solid. No horses and riders would be swept away, and no wagons would bog down.

Once they were across and had established their camp, Beale sent out the hunters. They were back in less than an hour with an antelope slung across their extra horse.

"Thicker'n fleas on a dog's back out there," one of the men said. "Easy shootin'."

They butchered the antelope, and soon Fargo heard the sizzle and pop of the meat being cooked. The smell made his mouth water as he looked out over the countryside to the west.

He could see low mountains and mesas, now changing color as the sun sank closer to the horizon. They would pose no obstacle to the expedition, nor would San Francisco Mountain, which loomed in the distance. Fargo thought they could make it there easily the day after they explored the canyon and set up camp at its base.

There was nothing out in the country ahead to delay them, Fargo thought. They would pass some interesting caves that Biggle would doubtless want to investigate, and Fargo supposed Beale would let him have a look at them. It wouldn't slow them down much if he did.

And then there was Manuelito. He could certainly slow them down, but Fargo was beginning to wonder if he'd been wrong about the Navajo all along. It seemed to Fargo that he'd have made some attempt by now to get his revenge if he had any intentions along those lines. But Indians could be patient, and maybe Manuelito was just waiting for exactly the right time and place.

Fargo thought again about the trip into Canyon Diablo, as the Spanish had named it. Devil's Canyon. Could be that Manuelito would think that was a good place for whatever he had planned. Fargo figured he'd find out tomorrow, one way or the other.

That night Fargo made his usual reconnoiter, encountering no one and nothing suspicious, but when he came back to his bedroll, he discovered that he had company.

"I was lonely," Sarah Gallagher said. "So I thought I'd pay you a visit."

"Does your brother know?"

"He's so worried about his maps that he can't think about anything else. He's with Cyrus Johnson now, and he'll be with him for a good while trying to get things straightened out."

Sarah was sitting by Fargo's bedroll. He dropped down beside her on the grass.

"What about Montgomery?"

"They don't want to include him in their little discussion. I think he must be part of the problem. In fact I know he is." Sarah paused. "Did you know that his daughter was spending some time with Private Slater?"

Fargo shrugged. "I saw them talking today."

"I don't like her. And I don't like that Slater, either. He's been spreading rumors about Hi Jolly having something to do with Private Vinson's death."

"Are you sure Slater's the one?"

"No. If I were, I'd go to Lieutenant Beale."

She put her hand out and toyed with the buttons on Fargo's shirt.

"But I didn't really come here to talk about Slater or the surveying problems."

Fargo allowed himself a thin smile.

"What did you come here to talk about?"

"I didn't come here to talk at all, Fargo, and I think you know it."

She undid the button she'd been fingering and slipped a hand inside his shirt. Fargo leaned forward and kissed her, and in a short time they were both out of their clothes.

Fargo went very slowly, as Sarah was still a bit skittish, though eager at the same time. Fargo wanted to help her recapture the feelings she'd had the previous night, and he teased her to the height of intensity twice before allowing his finger to slip into her wet crevice and give her the release she craved. Her climax shook her from the top of her head to the soles of her feet, but in only minutes she was ready to let Fargo have his turn.

She leaned over him and took him in her mouth. She was awkward, not nearly as practiced as Jane Montgomery. She used her tongue inexpertly, but Fargo could hardly complain. In seconds he was ready for his explosion.

Sarah seemed to realize it, and she stopped what she was doing to say, "I want you inside me, Fargo. Now. Please."

She lay back, and he entered her gently, but soon they were rocking together as if one of them was the camel and the other was the rider. Fargo came in one hot burst after another, and Sarah's interior muscles gripped him each time, coaxing more out of him until his supply was temporarily exhausted.

They lay together, the sweat of their exertions cooled by the night breeze.

"Did I mention that I don't like Jane Montgomery?" Sarah said after a while.

"You did, but you didn't say why."

"There's you, for one thing." Fargo moved beside her as if to sit up, and she put a hand on his chest, pushing him back down. "Oh, don't worry, Fargo. I was only teasing. I know I don't own you. I wouldn't even want to. You're a fine man to teach me certain things, but I know you'll never settle down. It's just not in you."

Fargo kept quiet. She was right, but there was no need to tell her so.

"What I don't like," Sarah went on, "is the way her father looks at her sometimes, and the way she talks to that Slater. It's just not right."

"There's not much we can do about any of that," Fargo said.

"I know, but that doesn't make me feel any better about it."

"I'll keep an eye on them," Fargo said.

"I know you will. That's why I mentioned it."

Fargo wondered if he was becoming her protector now rather than Randall. But he didn't say anything about that, either.

16

The next morning at daybreak the sky was covered in a pink haze in the west, but shortly afterward the haze burned away, and the sky was empty of clouds. The only thing that moved in it was a hawk. After sunup it was as if the countryside were sitting under a big inverted blue bowl.

"A fine day for a little exploring," Biggle said, pushing his glasses up on his nose. "Don't you agree, Tolliver?"

Tolliver agreed. He'd been very quiet since Vinson's death, but today he seemed to Fargo more like his usual self.

"And what about you, Sergeant Carter?" Biggle said.

Carter grunted, and Fargo could tell he wasn't as happy about exploring the canyon as Biggle and Tolliver were. They could tell, too.

"You could stay behind if you wanted to," Biggle told him. "I'm sure the lieutenant wouldn't mind, and Fargo will be protection enough for us. We're not likely to run into anything more dangerous than a rock or a plant."

Carter snorted. "The lieutenant told me to go, and that's that."

"Then let's get started," Fargo said, and the four of them moved out.

They were all riding horses, though Fargo thought that Tolliver, with his desert helmet on, would have looked at home on a camel. Fargo, however, was the only one of them who'd ridden a camel, and he wasn't sure what kind of terrain they might run into in the canyon. He wanted a mount he knew and trusted.

As they approached the canyon's mouth, Tolliver guided his horse over beside Fargo and Carter.

"There's something I've been thinking about," he said.

"That can be dangerous," Carter said. "But you better go ahead and tell us anyway, since that must be why you came over here."

"It's about Vinson," Tolliver said.

"What about him?" Fargo asked.

"It's the way he died. I said it had to be something that resulted from his broken leg. At the time I thought that had to be the case. Now I'm not so sure."

"What changed your mind?" Fargo said.

"I've thought of a way he could have been killed."

"Well, I can't think of one," Carter said. "If anybody'd killed him, somebody would have heard him yellin', even over all the snorin' that goes on."

"Not if there was no struggle," Tolliver said.

"Vinson would've struggled," Carter said. "He wouldn't let somebody kill him and not put up a fight. And besides, there weren't any marks on 'im."

"You're forgetting the back of his heel," Fargo said.

Tolliver nodded. "That's right."

"Nobody could kill him by scratchin' his heel."

"Remember Achilles?"

"Never heard of him. What regiment is he in?"

"Never mind. Vinson's heel is not what killed him. But I think it might have been scraped and bruised when he kicked it against the bottom of the wagon."

Carter pushed up the brim of his hat and gave Tolliver a skeptical look.

"Why would he do that?"

"Because somebody was killing him. Or rather, two people were. If two people held him, he couldn't struggle, and one of them could smother him easily enough. There wouldn't be any signs for us to find."

"Besides the heel," Fargo said.

"Yes. Besides the heel. And that wouldn't have made much noise at all."

"And you think that's what happened?"

"I think it could have. I don't know that it did, and even if I was certain, there wouldn't be any way I could prove it."

"I can sure as hell think of two candidates for the hangin' if you could," Carter said.

So could Fargo. He remembered what Vinson had said to him about Slater and Logan, and he wondered if Vinson had mentioned something similar to any of his other visitors. If he had, the word would have gotten back to Slater and Logan soon enough, and they might well have decided to take care of Vinson before his loose talk about them got someone all too interested in their pasts. Fargo was liking less and less the fact that Jane was associating with them. They were dangerous, and she could get hurt.

"What are we gonna do about this?" Carter asked. "We need to tell the lieutenant."

"I'll tell him," Tolliver said. "If you think it's the thing to do."

Both Carter and Fargo said that it was, though Fargo didn't think there was anything Beale could do about it because of the lack of any proof other than their suspicions.

Tolliver said he'd talk to Beale after they got back to camp and rode off to start classifying plants. Biggle was already well into the canyon, chipping rocks and drawing pictures of the strata. Every now and then Fargo could hear the ring of his hammer on stone.

"Reckon there's any gold in here?" Carter asked Fargo later as they rode slowly along, looking up at the striated walls of the canyon that rose high above them.

"Biggle didn't seem to think so when I talked to him about it," Fargo said. "He didn't believe those stories of Spanish gold, either."

Carter looked over at the river, more like a creek, that flowed through the bottom of the canyon.

"I've heard some of those stories. They say those old explorers came into this part of the country and looked all of it over. There were supposed to be whole cities of gold out here."

"Nobody's ever found them," Fargo said.

"Maybe old Coronado and his men passed this way."

"And brought all their gold with them."

"Well, that's what they say. Maybe they were trying to hide it from the Apaches to the east of us. But I never figured out what they gained by doin' that. You get away from the Apaches, but you wind up with the Navajos. I never saw that much to choose between them."

"Manuelito's people haven't given you much trouble."

Carter pulled back on the reins and stopped his horse. Fargo reined in the Ovaro beside him.

"Manuelito's done us no harm because he hasn't had a reason. Now that he's got one, thanks to Slater and Logan, he damn sure could hurt us. You think he's just after you, but what if you're wrong? What if his whole bunch is out there just waitin' for a chance to fill us full of arrows?"

"Too much trouble, that's why. Manuelito saw what we could do, and he saw that his men and horses didn't like the camels. But he could come alone and get one man."

"Maybe, but they won't be surprised by the camels again. You think he snuck into camp and got Vinson?"

"No," Fargo said. "I think Slater and Logan did."

"Yeah," Carter said. "Me, too."

The day went well. Biggle had more than enough rocks and strata to keep him happy, and Tolliver filled his notebook with sketches of plants.

But Fargo couldn't rid himself of the nagging notion that they were being watched. There was nothing he could pinpoint, just an itch between his shoulder blades, and an occasional glimpse of a motion up on the rim of the canyon, a glimpse so fleeting that he couldn't swear that he'd really seen anything at all.

And there was an encounter with a rattlesnake that unsettled Biggle considerably but that resulted in no harm except, as Biggle put it, a slight soiling of the trousers.

Carter laughed at that, knowing that Biggle was kidding, and wondered out loud what might happen if one of the camels had a run-in with a rattler.

"Probably eat the critter," he said, answering his own question. "Or stomp it flat. I don't think one of them animals would be scared of anything."

"Not as scared as I was, anyway," Biggle said.

"You didn't find any gold, did you?" Carter asked him.

Biggle laughed. "No, and I didn't expect to. There's no gold in this country, as I once told Fargo."

"Could be Spanish gold."

Biggle looked at Fargo. "Have you been talking to the sergeant?"

"He'd already heard the stories," Fargo said. "I imagine everybody has. And not from me."

"Well, he can forget them. We'll not see any gold on this expedition."

Carter nodded, but he didn't look convinced. Fargo supposed it was hard to give up on the idea of hidden gold once you'd heard the stories about it. It was a lot more comforting to believe in it being hidden out there somewhere, and to think maybe you'd even be the one to find it, than to accept the idea that it didn't exist at all.

It had been a long day, and it was getting dark in the canyon. Fargo said that it was time to head back to the camp.

Biggle and Tolliver were reluctant to leave the canyon, but they didn't want to be there after dark. And they didn't want to miss their supper. They agreed that it was time to go.

By the time they arrived at the camp, the food had already been cooked. More antelope steak, and Fargo had no complaints about it, though his was cooked a little more than he would have liked.

When he was finished, he made his usual circuit of the camp and returned to his bedroll, halfway expecting Sarah Gallagher to be there waiting for him.

She wasn't, and Fargo was a bit disappointed. However, he knew he could use the rest and the sleep, so he unrolled his blanket and lay down on the ground.

He was asleep before he could think of Sarah again.

Randall Gallagher woke Fargo up before dawn.

He shook Fargo's shoulder and was more than a little surprised and frightened when he suddenly found his hand pinned to the ground and the barrel of Fargo's big .45 stuck up against the bridge of his nose.

"It's j-just m-me, Fargo. R-Randall Gallagher. You don't have to shoot."

"You ought to be more careful about how you wake a man," Fargo said, lowering the hammer on the .45 and putting it back under the blanket that had pillowed his head. "What's your trouble?"

"It's Sarah," Gallagher said. "She's gone."

Fargo sat up. "Gone where?"

"I don't know. That's why I came to you. She was supposed to be in the wagon, asleep, and I thought that's where she was. I was working on some maps with Clyde until late last night, and when I came in I was careful not to wake her. Now I'm not sure she was there at all."

"When did you notice she was gone?"

"Just now. I wasn't sleeping well, and I got up to walk around the wagon to try and relax. Sarah wasn't there."

The first thing Fargo wanted to know was whether anyone else was missing, so before long the whole camp was roused.

Sure enough, Slater and Logan were gone, too.

17

Randall was distraught. "Why would they take Sarah? She'll be so frightened that she might die."

Fargo thought that Randall was wrong about that. Sarah might be frightened, but not as frightened as she would have been a few days before. She had more confidence in herself now, but Fargo wasn't in a position to explain that to Randall.

"The question is," said Lieutenant Beale, "where did they go?"

Tolliver had pulled Fargo aside after supper the previous evening and told him that he'd spoken to Beale about their suspicions regarding Vinson's death. Fargo wondered if Beale had confronted Slater and Logan, which might explain their absence. But not Sarah's, though it seemed likely that the two things were connected.

"I can track them as soon as it gets light," Fargo said. He didn't think either Logan or Slater knew enough about hiding tracks to throw off a trailsman. "You can start on toward San Francisco Mountain later, but wait until around noon. I don't want you coming along and scaring Slater and Logan off."

Beale agreed that it would be a good idea to delay the expedition's departure.

"I'll go with you," Carter told Fargo. "Those two skunks are my responsibility."

Hi Jolly was standing nearby. He said, "I advise you to take a camel. They are more dependable than horses, and you might need a mount for Miss Gallagher should you find her. You can take Samuel, as he knows her."

115

"You won't need a camel," Private Spence said as he joined the group. "There's three horses missing. I'd say Miss Gallagher was on one of 'em. If you get her back, she'll already have a mount."

"She wouldn't go off with those men," Randall said. "Not Sarah."

"Maybe not willingly," Fargo said, knowing his words would do little to comfort Randall, who looked at him bleakly.

"I'll have a look at the tracks in a few minutes," Fargo said. "That should tell us something."

Before he had a chance, Jane Montgomery asked Fargo if she could have a word with him. They stepped over near one of the wagons to talk. Oddly enough, she and her father seemed, if anything, more upset than Randall about Sarah's disappearance.

"You have to find them," Jane said. "Do you think there's a chance Sarah might have gone with those two because she wanted to?"

"No," Fargo said. "She didn't want to go."

"You sound awfully certain."

"I am."

Fargo didn't want to explain to Jane why he was sure. It wasn't the kind of story Sarah would've wanted to have spread around.

"Are you sure she's the one you're worried about?" Fargo asked. "I thought you might be a little sweet on Slater, yourself."

Jane gave him a wry grin. "Why, Mr. Fargo, could it be that you're jealous?"

"Not a bit," Fargo told her. "But you could say I'm curious about why you and Slater seemed to have your heads together so much lately."

Jane's grin changed quickly to a hard frown.

"That's private business, Fargo. Now if you want to run after that little floozy, you'd better get started."

Fargo left her standing beside a wagon, but he had an uneasy feeling about the whole encounter, as if there was more going on than he was aware of. He told himself that he couldn't worry about it now. He went to find Carter, who was waiting with the horses.

116

The first thing Fargo did was check for tracks, and he found three sets leading off to the west.

"Won't be easy to track 'em on this hard ground," Carter said. "And where the hell would they be goin', anyway?"

Fargo thought he had an idea about that.

"There are some caves between here and that mountain." He pointed to San Francisco Mountain, which was just then beginning to catch the first rays of the morning sun. "I think we'll find them there."

"What makes you think so?"

"If you were a Spaniard in this country, and if some Navajos were after you, where would you hide your gold?"

"In some caves, I guess. Why didn't you just say so? Let's get goin'."

Fargo and Carter rode over a rolling countryside that was covered with grass that waved in the breeze.

"Could pasture a lot of cattle here," Carter said. "They'd have to go back to the river for water, though."

After a few miles, they passed between two tall sandstone rocks. There were some words scratched on them, and Fargo thought they might have been Spanish names.

"Then those fellas with the gold did come this way," Carter said.

"The Spanish were here long before we ever were," Fargo said. "And the Mexicans after that. But that doesn't mean they were carrying gold."

"I'm bettin' Slater and Logan think they were and that they're at those caves right now."

"So am I," Fargo said.

It was a little after midmorning when Fargo and Carter came to the caves. They lined the side of a rocky ridge, and there were too many of them for Fargo to count. They were on two levels, one under the top of the ridge and another below. There was a narrow ledge in front of the caves on the first level that would make walking between them easy enough.

"Lordy," Carter said as they approached the caves. "How did those things get there?"

The caves were shallow for the most part, and not very well protected from the weather. The ground below them was littered with piles of volcanic rocks, and the rocks were stacked all along the ridge, sometimes as high as the topmost openings.

Before they got too close to the caves, Fargo said, "We'd better leave the horses in those trees over there."

"Where do you reckon that Logan and Slater left theirs?" Carter said. "I sure as hell don't see 'em."

Fir trees pushed up through the rock all along the top of the ridge, and Fargo said that the horses might be up there. Or in some other clump of the trees along the bottom.

"If Slater and Logan are up there, they can see us comin'," Carter said. "There's lots of open ground between us and them caves."

"Not much we can do about that," Fargo said.

"Be careful, is all. But you were plannin' to do that, I guess. They might've already seen us, though."

"Too late to worry about that," Fargo said. "Let's hide the horses."

They did, and from the cover of the trees Fargo scanned the ridge. The caves stretched as far as he could see in both directions, and he guessed there might have been as many as a thousand of them, large, small, and every size in between.

"Take 'em a month to search all those caves," Carter said. "Maybe more. I'd look in the big ones first, though, if it was me doin' the lookin'."

Most of the bigger caves were a good way off to the left, maybe a quarter of a mile or more, and Fargo thought he might have glimpsed a movement in one of them. He pointed it out to Carter and said, "Let's work our way down in that direction."

Sheltering as best they could in the trees and behind piles of rock, they eased toward the cave where Fargo had seen something. When they were about halfway there, Carter said, "Hold on, Fargo. Look at that."

He pointed to the trees on the rim of the ridge, and this time there was no question about it. Something was moving in them.

"Must be the horses," Carter said. "I can't see 'em, though."

Neither could Fargo, but he was sure that had to be what was moving around. Men wouldn't have been so careless. But if the horses were there, the men had to be nearby.

And, of course, they were.

About that time, Slater came out of one of the upper caves and looked around. Fargo and Carter ducked behind the rocks, and he didn't see them. He said something that Fargo didn't hear, and Logan came out of the cave behind him. They stood there talking things over, though Fargo couldn't make out any of the words. Then they walked along a ledge leading to the next cave and disappeared inside it.

"Where's the girl?" Carter whispered.

Fargo didn't know, but he had an idea that the two men had tied Sarah up and left her with the horses or in one of the caves. They wouldn't want to have to worry about her as they were doing their exploring.

"What're we gonna to now?" Carter said.

Fargo thought it over and said, "We'll go on down to that pathway there." It was about fifty yards away and led up the side of the ridge. Fargo pointed to it, and Carter nodded. "If we get to it without being seen, we'll climb up and go along the edge until we get to Slater and Logan."

"Better check in the caves for the girl as we go."

Fargo nodded and moved away, crouching to stay behind the rocks. They reached the pathway just as Slater and Logan emerged from the cave they'd been exploring. Fargo ducked behind a scrubby green bush, and Carter followed.

Once again, the two men on the ledge talked things over briefly before moving into the next cave. When they were out of sight, Fargo stepped out from behind the tree and went up the path, trying to keep the thin soil from crunching under his boot soles. He didn't look behind him, but he knew Carter was there. He wasn't as quiet as Fargo was.

When they reached the ledge, they went into the nearest cave. The entrance was high enough for Fargo to go inside without stooping, and it was about ten feet wide. So there was plenty of light. Someone many years ago had carved out small storage spaces in the walls, which had been plastered with mud. The cave was only about twelve feet deep, and Fargo could see at once that there was no gold hidden inside. And there was no sign of Sarah Gallagher.

"Here's what we'll do," Fargo told Carter. "I'll go straight on to the cave where Slater and Logan are. You come along behind and check the caves we pass for Sarah. And watch my back."

"Ain't nobody behind us."

Fargo wasn't so sure of that. He still felt they were being watched, the way he had in the canyon on the previous day.

"You're forgetting Manuelito," he said.

"You think he's here?"

"I don't know that he is, but I don't know that he's not. So we have to be as careful as if he was out there."

"Guess you're right. I'll keep my eyes peeled."

Fargo nodded and left the cave, his .45 in his hand.

18

The Trailsman walked swiftly along the ledge. Just before he got to the cave where Slater and Logan were, he heard voices and stopped.

"Not a damn thing in this one, either."

That was Slater, Fargo thought. It seemed as if they weren't having any luck.

"No, damn it," Logan said. "Nobody told us there were so many of these damn caves. We could spend a month here and not look in all of 'em."

"We're not going to stay that long. Beale will be here by late afternoon, and he might send somebody out ahead to look for us before that."

"We should never have taken that Gallagher bitch with us. Should've just killed her and had done with it."

"If we'd done that, Beale would've hunted us to the end of the earth. What we should've done was left her there at the camp."

"We couldn't do that. We had to take her. It was her own fault she was wandering around in the dark. She saw us, and she would've caused us trouble."

"She's caused us trouble already. You think Beale would hunt us forever if we killed her? What do you think he'll do now that she's missing?"

"The hell with it. We gotta find that gold and get our asses out of here."

"Beale won't be the only one who's pissed off."

"That's why we gotta hurry. There's nothing here. Let's move on to the next cave."

That was Fargo's cue to take over. He stepped into

sight of the cave entrance and said, "No need to move. Just stay right where you are."

"Shit," Logan said.

Slater was standing behind Logan, and he didn't say a word. Instead he pushed Logan in the back as hard as he could.

Slater was smaller than Logan, but he was strong, and he sent the bigger man stumbling forward toward Fargo, his arms windmilling wildly as he tried to get his balance. His face wore a look of sheer terror mixed with surprise.

Fargo jumped out of the way. Logan tried to get a grip with his boots on the rim of the ledge, but he didn't have a chance. He was leaning too far forward. Loose gravel slid under him and he pitched over the edge. The fall into the pile of rocks below wasn't a long one, but as soon as Logan hit the rocks, Fargo heard the distinctive sound of rattlers.

Fargo didn't look down to see what had happened to Logan because Slater was moving the whole time. He bent over and scooped a handful of dirt, which he threw in Fargo's direction while drawing his pistol. He triggered off a couple of quick shots, missing Fargo completely. But while Fargo was waiting for the dust to settle, Slater ran out of the cave and into the next one.

From where he was standing on the ledge, Fargo was able to put two shots into the roof of the cave and let them ricochet around inside it. He didn't think he could kill Slater, but he might be able to disable him.

"Goddammit, Fargo!" Slater said. "You son of a bitch!"

"Got a mouth on him, don't he?" Carter said from behind Fargo. "The girl's not in any of those caves, in case you were wonderin'."

"Thanks for looking. Right now I'm more worried about Slater."

"What about Logan?" Carter said, looking down at the trooper who was screaming and trying to get up from where he lay in the rocks. There was a four-foot rattler hanging from his right cheek.

Fargo didn't much care one way or the other. He said, "You can go down there and help him out if you want to."

"I don't think so. Let him help himself. Besides, that

122

little son of a bitch Slater would just as soon shoot me in the back as not. Put a few more shots into that cave. You might hit him."

Fargo did as Carter suggested. One of the bullets spanged into something metallic, but Slater didn't say a thing. Fargo knew he was trying to decide what to do.

Slater didn't have many choices. He could stay in the cave without food or water until he either died, which would take a while, or until he decided to give up.

Or he could come out.

And that's what he did. He came out at a dead run, but not down the ledge. He ran straight ahead, and when he hit the rim of the ledge, he launched himself forward in a long jump.

Fargo could see what Slater hoped to do. There was a patch of open ground down below, and if the trooper could land there without snapping his spine or breaking some other important bones, he might have a chance to get away.

Or he might have if Fargo hadn't shot him in midleap.

Slater cried out and twisted. He hit the ground flat on his face and lay there, sprawled out, his arms thrown out as if he might be trying to fly.

Below Fargo and Carter, in the rocks, Logan had managed to get to his feet. The rattler still had its fangs hung in his cheek, and he had hold of the snake with both hands around its middle as if trying to stop its thrashing. The tip of its tail still whirred and whipped from side to side, and Logan was still yelling.

"Shoot the poor son of a bitch," Carter said. "It's about the only chance he's got."

"I'd have to reload," Fargo said. "And he doesn't have a chance at all."

As Fargo spoke, three more rattlers slithered out of the crevices in the pile of rocks and struck at Logan. Two of them hit his boots, but one launched itself a bit higher and got him in the calf. Logan fell over backward and hit his head on a rock with a sickening sound. He stopped screaming.

"Lucky bastard," Carter said. "He'll be out till he dies." He looked over to where Slater lay stretched out in the sun. "I think that one's already done for."

But just as he said it, Slater moved as if he was trying to pull himself forward.

"We need to look for Miss Gallagher," Carter said. "Even if he is still alive."

"We'll find her after we have a talk with Slater," Fargo told him.

They went back down the ledge to the path and walked to the bottom of the ridge. By the time they got to Slater, he'd moved about three feet. The toes of his boots had left two lines in the gravelly soil behind him.

Fargo stuck out a foot and nudged him. "Slater?"

"Go to hell," Slater said.

His voice was so weak that Fargo barely heard him. The side of his blouse was dark, soaked with blood.

"Where's Sarah Gallagher?" Fargo said.

"Go to hell."

"That's where you're headed, Slater. Why did you tell folks that Hi Jolly had killed Vinson?"

"Didn't."

Slater never looked up at Fargo, never looked to either side. He stared straight ahead as if he saw something that was visible only to him, and he inched along as he struggled to reach it.

"You and Slater killed him, didn't you?"

"We never."

Slater gained another inch on whatever it was he was trying to get to.

"There's no use in lyin' now," Carter said. "You ain't gonna make it, Slater."

"I'll get there."

He moved another inch forward.

"You can tell us the truth," Fargo said. "We'll do what we can for you."

"Told you the truth," Slater said.

He lunged straight ahead for about half a foot and closed his hands around nothing.

"Got it," he said, and then blood ran out of his mouth and he died.

"Little bastard was a liar right till the end," Carter said. "We can bury him later, when the expedition gets here. Better have a look at Logan."

Logan was dead, too. The snake that had bitten him

in the calf was gone, but the one affixed to his cheek was still there, writhing in Logan's death grip.

"You gonna kill it?" Carter said.

"Leave it," Fargo said. "If it doesn't get itself loose, we'll kill it later. Right now, we'd better look for Sarah."

"Better reload that pistol first. Never know what we'll run into."

"You're right about that," Fargo said.

They climbed up the path to the top of the ridge and went to the copse of fir trees where they thought they'd seen the movement of the horses. Three horses were picketed there, but there was no sign of Sarah.

"You think she's down there in one of the caves?" Carter said.

Fargo hoped not. If she was, they'd have to look for her, and that might take quite a while. Besides, now that he thought about it, he couldn't see Slater and Logan trying to get her down to one of the caves. She would have struggled and made it hard on them if they'd done it.

"She has to be around here somewhere," Fargo said. "We'll just have to find her."

"That should not be hard," Manuelito said, stepping out from behind a tree. "I have her here."

19

Manuelito was short and stocky, and his thick black hair was hacked off short. The puckered scar on his chest stood out like a thick worm that had crawled under his skin, and Fargo wondered how long the Navajo had been laid up before he recovered from the Spanish musket ball. It must have been quite a while.

"You are the one they call the Trailsman," Manuelito said to Fargo.

"That's right, and you're Kin' hozhoni. Manuelito. This fella with me is Sergeant Carter."

"I guess we can consider ourselves formally introduced without havin' to shake on it," Carter said.

Manuelito didn't smile. He was holding an old Spanish musket in the crook of his arm, and it was plain that he wouldn't hesitate to fire it.

"We want the woman," Fargo said.

"And I need to avenge the death of my cousin, Short Knife. You are the one who killed him."

"You've had your revenge," Fargo said. "There are two dead men down there at the foot of the ridge. They're the ones who caused your cousin's death."

"You are the one," Manuelito said, "who shot him."

Fargo saw something moving in the brush behind Manuelito. He figured it was Sarah, but he didn't call the Navajo's attention to it.

"Yeah, I shot him. I can't deny it. But it was in battle, and he had his chance at me. Those two dead men were the ones who cheated him in the horse race. If it hadn't been for them, you wouldn't have attacked the expedition, and Short Knife would be alive right now."

"How do I know that those two men are the ones you say they are?" Manuelito asked.

"You'd just have to take my word for it. If you've heard of the Trailsman, you know I don't make a habit of lying."

"It is said that you are one of the few truthful white men," Manuelito admitted. "But that does not mean I believe you."

Behind him, Sarah was emerging from the trees. She had a large rock in one hand.

"I am afraid that even a truthful white man may lie when he thinks it means his life," Manuelito said.

He moved the musket to level it at Fargo, and the Trailsman said, "You can't hit both of us with that."

"I will kill the old man with my knife after you are dead," Manuelito said.

"Who the hell you callin' old?" Carter said. "Why, I can whip your ass with one hand tied behind me."

Fargo knew that Carter saw Sarah, too, and that the sergeant was talking to keep Manuelito's attention.

"He's old, but he's tough," Fargo said. "You'd never beat him, Manuelito."

Manuelito almost smiled. "You see? Even a truthful white man will lie. I will beat him easily, and you know it is so. But you will not be here to see it."

"You never know," Fargo said, and Sarah hit Manuelito in the back of the head with the rock.

The Navajo wasn't knocked out, but he was staggered, and he lost his grip on the musket. As it fell to the ground, Fargo jumped across the space that separated them, drawing his pistol as he did.

Before Manuelito could recover from the blow on his head, Fargo was standing in front of him with the barrel of the .45 stuck up under the Navajo's chin.

"Game's over," Fargo said.

"I wasn't scared," Sarah said. "Thanks to you, Fargo. No matter what Slater and Logan said, I knew they couldn't do anything to me that I couldn't recover from." She paused. "But that doesn't mean I'm not glad they're dead."

"Too bad Manuelito wasn't glad," Carter said. "He

might not have got himself conked in the head and hog-tied if he had been."

"I'd been trying to get loose ever since Slater and Logan tied me up," Sarah said. "They stuck an old sock in my mouth and tied it there, too. That was the worst thing of all. They must never have washed their feet. Or their socks."

Her face twisted in disgust at the thought of it.

"But they didn't tie very good knots," Carter said.

"They were good enough. They got me early last night, and it took me all this time to get loose."

She stuck out her wrists for Carter to see. They were red and skinned and bleeding.

"The thing is that you did get loose," Fargo said. "Just in time, I'd say."

"Manuelito said he wouldn't hurt me. But I didn't believe him."

"I think you could believe him. He's a lot of things, but he's not a liar. Isn't that right, Manuelito."

Manuelito, who was tied hand and foot and propped against the trunk of a fir tree, spat into the dirt.

"There's no call for that," Fargo said. "You got caught off guard, but there's no disgrace in that."

"You will kill me while I am tied. There is disgrace in that. For me, and for you."

"Nobody's going to kill you," Fargo told him. "We're going to let you go."

Manuelito said nothing, but the look in his eyes said that he thought Fargo was lying for sure this time.

"All you have to do is go back home and tell your tribe that you've avenged Short Knife's death," Fargo said. "And that there's no more revenge to be had."

"How can they believe me?"

"Because of what I told you. Those two men down below us are the cause of all the trouble, and they're dead. You didn't kill them, but I did."

"You had a little help from them snakes," Carter said.

"That's right. Even the rattlers didn't like Logan. So you can rest easy about your revenge, Manuelito."

Manuelito didn't look convinced.

"And we won't tell anybody it was a woman that hit

you in the head with a rock," Carter said. "If that's what's worryin' you."

"It is not. She hit me unfairly from behind."

"I guess it's all settled, then," Fargo said. "Let him loose, Carter."

Carter moved the Navajo away from the tree and untied the ropes that held him.

"We're even going to give you your musket," Fargo said. "It's not loaded, though."

"Why are you doing this?" Manuelito said, rubbing his wrists, which were in better shape than Sarah's.

"Because we're not your enemies. If you had any enemies, they're lying dead down there."

"My cousin was cheated by those two? It is certain?"

"They're the ones. They won't be cheating anybody else."

"And we can return to the fort for the racing and the gambling?"

"That's up to the commanding officer, but I don't see why not."

"We will not be cheated?"

That was a good question, and Fargo wished he could tell Manuelito that the cheating was over for good. But there was no way he could promise that.

"I hope you won't," Fargo said.

"If we are cheated again, there will be trouble. Much more trouble than two dead men."

"I'll tell them what you've said. Bring his horse, Carter."

Carter led Manuelito's horse to him, and the Navajo mounted.

"I believe you are a just man, Fargo," he said. "If all whites were like you, things would be better between us."

He turned his horse's head and rode away.

"You think he's gonna leave you alone?" Carter asked as they watched Manuelito disappear.

Fargo nodded. "I think he will. He's satisfied now. He might even trust us a little."

"What'll we do about Slater and Logan?"

"We'll let Lieutenant Beale worry about them when

129

he gets here. He should be getting on the way about now."

"And we'll just wait for him?"

"We'll see about that. But right now there's something I need to have a look at," Fargo said, thinking about the metallic sound of a ricochet.

The last cave that Slater had ducked into was no bigger than any of the others, nor was it any more interesting, except for one thing. Lying in the back against the wall were a metal helmet and breastplate. They may have been highly polished once, but now they were darkly tarnished. Spiderwebs covered much of them. They were worn by a skeleton, whose sword and spurs were still there as well, along with remnants of his clothing.

"I'll be damned," Carter said, "beggin' your pardon for the language, Miss Gallagher. Those stories were true. The Spaniards did make it this far, after all."

"One of them did," Fargo said. "That doesn't mean any of the others ever came here, or that this one had any gold with him."

"Reckon that gold is what Slater was searchin' for when he died?"

Fargo shrugged, and Carter said, "We oughta look for it. The gold, I mean."

"There's no gold in here," Sarah said. "There's nothing except that dead man and his armor."

"Could be buried."

Carter took a step toward the armor and put out his hand as if to touch it, but before he could, they all heard an all-too-familiar whirring sound.

Carter stepped back, tucking his arm to his side.

"Those son of bitches are everywhere," he said. "Pardon my language again, Miss Gallagher."

"I don't blame you one bit," Sarah said, backing out of the cave.

"It's no wonder Slater came flying outta there the way he did," Carter said. "He near about wound up like his friend Logan. Not that what did happen to him was much better."

Fargo stood in the entrance and looked around the

cave. It was no different from the few others he'd seen, with the plastered walls and the niches for food or whatever else might have been stored there by a people now long departed for some other place.

The Trailsman wondered how the Spaniard had come to be there and whether anyone else, other than Slater, of course, had ever seen his bones.

But the Spaniard wasn't anything to Fargo, who doubted that a single man would have brought any gold with him to this place. Fargo also doubted that there had been anyone with the man, else they would have buried him rather than leaving him to his fate in the open cave.

The rattler whirred again, but Fargo still couldn't see it. He thought it must be coiled within the rib cage of the skeleton, hidden by the breastplate. Fargo wondered if it was a descendant of some other rattler who had lived in that very spot and had long ago given a fatal bite to a man who was sheltering in the cave from some sudden and unexpected storm.

"There's no gold here," Fargo said. "Nothing but a snake. Let's see about Logan."

He walked to the ledge and looked down. The snake was no longer clinging to Logan's cheek, having managed to slither out of his grip and disappear.

Carter looked up and out toward the east. "Reckon how close to us the expedition is."

"Let's go find out," Fargo said. "No need for us to wait, not now."

20

The expedition wasn't far, and after meeting up with Fargo and the others it went on to the caves. Lieutenant Beale called a halt there so that a burial detail could be sent to take care of Slater and Logan. Fargo warned the men who'd be going about the snakes.

Beale was pleased that Fargo had taken care of things with Manuelito and the two dead troopers so neatly.

"I just hope that this affair won't put a stain on our accomplishment when we reach California," Beale said. "I want our California camel corps to be known for the honesty and integrity of its men."

"Then you'd better do your best to keep out people like those two they're burying," Fargo said. "They weren't the best men in any corps."

"I don't know how such men get into the army," Beale said. "I would hope that they're the exception rather than the rule."

Fargo said he thought that was the case. "You can see that the rest of the men you have with you are a cut above those two."

"That's certainly true," Beale said, looking cheered by the thought. "And the camels are doing exceptionally well. The California camel corps will be a huge success. I'm sure of it."

Fargo had his doubts. As far as he could tell, nobody but Beale and Hi Jolly really liked the idea of using camels. The mules and horses still had to be picketed somewhere away from them, and the men weren't taking to them any better than the animals. Even the men who'd been with Beale all the way from Texas didn't seem to have grown to like the camels any better than the ones who started the trip at Fort Defiance. But maybe things would work out for Beale, Fargo thought. If he had powerful backers in Washington, it was possible.

Hi Jolly told Fargo that he was not sorry to hear that Slater and Logan had died.

"I believe that they were trying to cause me trouble because I do not believe as they did," he said.

Fargo said that he wasn't sure the two men had believed in much of anything, except maybe gold. He kept thinking of the way Slater had struggled forward toward something even as he died. Fargo was pretty sure it hadn't been heaven.

"I couldn't sleep, so I got up to walk around," Sarah said by way of explanation.

She didn't look at Fargo when she said it, and he thought maybe he knew where she'd been headed for some relaxing exercise to help her sleep.

"I ran into Slater and Logan by accident," she continued, "and they just grabbed me. I told them to let me go, but they said I'd be a danger to them. I had no idea what they were talking about."

"They were sneaking off to find some gold," Fargo said. "At least I think that's what they were doing. They didn't want you to alert anybody."

"I had no intention of doing that."

"They didn't know."

"I wasn't afraid," Sarah said. "I thought I would be, but I wasn't. I knew I'd get loose some way or other."

"Good thing for us you did," Fargo said.

"Amen," Carter said.

Randall Gallagher was effusive in thanking Fargo and Carter for the rescue of his sister, but Fargo pointed out that it had been Sarah who'd rescued them.

"That's God's truth," Carter said. "Hadn't been for her, me and Fargo'd probably be lyin' up there on top of that ridge with nobody to keep us company but a passel of rattlesnakes."

"Sarah was amazingly brave," Randall said. "I can't understand it. A situation like that, those two men, the things they must have said and thought about doing to her. She should have been terrified."

"You don't have to worry about her," Carter assured him. "That gal's got sand."

"I just wish I knew where she got it," Randall said, but Fargo kept quiet on that subject.

After the burials, the expedition had to travel double time to get to the spot Fargo had planned to camp by nightfall. But the going was easy, and while they didn't make it before sunset, they arrived just as the stars were coming out in the sky over San Francisco Mountain. It wasn't a big mountain. Fargo had seen plenty that were bigger. Nevertheless, it was impressive enough in its setting, but even at that it didn't amount to much of a barrier to their travel.

When he'd had supper, Fargo spread his bedroll away from the camp. He was getting ready to scout things out when Jane Montgomery showed up. Fargo had more or less been expecting her. The long braid of her heavy hair hung down her back, and she stood with her hands planted on her hips as she looked at Fargo.

"Well," she said, "you saved Sarah from a fate worse than death. I guess you're proud of yourself."

"Not so proud," Fargo said. "I didn't really save her from anything, and I had to kill a man that maybe didn't deserve it."

"I heard you killed two of them."

"I didn't kill Logan. Rattlers did. That was his partner's fault."

Fargo remembered the look of fear and surprise on Logan's face when Slater had pushed him out of the cave.

"I wonder if they found what they were looking for," Jane said.

"I guess we'll never know about that," Fargo said.

"Maybe not. I suppose it doesn't matter. They're still dead either way."

Uninvited, Jane walked over and sat down on Fargo's

blanket. She patted a place beside her and asked Fargo if he didn't want to rest while they talked.

"I need to have a look around the camp," he said.

"What would you be looking for? From what I hear, Manuelito had been following us all this time, but you took care of him, too. There shouldn't be anything else to worry about."

Fargo wasn't so sure about that, but he sat down beside Jane anyway.

"I had some help with Manuelito," he said. "He didn't really want to kill me, anyway. He was after Logan and Slater. He just didn't know it."

"But you convinced him."

"Yeah, you might say that."

Jane moved a little closer to Fargo. Their shoulders touched.

"They're saying that Slater and Logan were looking for gold in those caves."

"You keep coming back to what they were looking for," Fargo said.

"Somebody said that there was a suit of Spanish armor in one of the caves."

Fargo wondered who had talked. He figured it was Carter. Fargo hadn't asked him or Sarah to keep quiet about what they'd seen.

"That's all it was," Fargo said. "Armor. And a skeleton."

"Nothing else? You're sure?"

"If you're still thinking about gold, you can forget it. There were some snakes, though. Too many of them to suit me."

"Slater and Logan believed there was gold," Jane said. Her voice was confident.

"So that's what you and Slater talked about. I should have known."

Jane moved away from Fargo and gave him a cold look.

"I didn't talk to him about gold. I was just being friendly. I talk to a lot of people."

"I know that," Fargo said. "You were mighty nice to Vinson before he died."

Jane moved back closer to Fargo. He felt the warmth

of her flesh though their clothing as their shoulders touched again.

"I can be even friendlier to you than I ever was to Vinson or Slater," she said.

Fargo knew that, too, and when she turned to kiss him, he was ready.

She broke off the kiss and unbuttoned her shirt. Then she lifted Fargo's hands and put them on her firm breasts. Her nipples branded his palms.

"I need you, Fargo," she said. "Now."

She slithered out of her pants like a snake, and Fargo thought she might be as dangerous as a rattler in some ways. In moments she was completely nude. Her pale skin gleamed in the darkness, and her hard nipples stuck out like rifle balls.

Fargo said, "What about your father?"

Jane looked over her shoulder, then back at Fargo.

"We're alone here. He won't know."

As he peeled off his clothing, Fargo thought about just what Jane's father may or may not know. There were a lot of other things to think about, but at the moment they all slipped Fargo's mind, and he concentrated on Jane.

She came to him and pressed up against him, mashing her breasts to him and letting him feel the full length of his bone-hard shaft against her stomach.

"You're as ready as I am, Fargo," she said, lying back on the blanket, her knees spread. "Give it to me now."

Fargo gave it to her, sliding in all the way at the first stroke. He remained still for a while, letting her feel him inside her, but she was impatient and began agitating her hips beneath him. She established a rhythm he couldn't resist, and he began to thrust in and out, using long, slow strokes that drove her to a pitch of excitement that he found hard to match.

She wrapped her legs around him and pulled him deeply inside her, holding him there while her hips churned and she ground herself against him. Her fingernails dug into his back.

After a few seconds she heaved under him, urging him to begin thrusting, and this time he used short fast strokes that tingled the tip of his rod and brought Jane to a such a peak that she could no longer hold back. She bucked under him like an unbroken pony as her pleasure spasms wracked her body.

Just as she was about to subside, Fargo gave her several more swift strokes, and she started all over again. But this time Fargo joined her and he released himself into her in long, hot bursts.

When they had both exhausted themselves, they lay back on the blanket and were quiet. Finally Jane said, "You're much of a man, Fargo. If anyone could find that Spanish gold, it would be you."

"I told you," Fargo said. "There isn't any gold."

"I know, and I believe you. I'm not sure I'd believe anyone else."

"You believed Slater."

"We didn't talk about the gold." Jane sat up and started to get dressed. "I told you that."

Fargo didn't say any more, and when she was gone, he put on his own clothes and went to look around. He didn't find anything or see anyone other than the troopers on sentry duty at the edge of the camp, and they didn't see him.

Fargo hadn't quite figured out some of the things that had happened on the expedition so far. He wasn't sure what kind of danger they represented to the expedition, if any, but they didn't seem to fit any kind of pattern. And that bothered him.

He went back to his blanket and lay down with his hands behind his head, the fingers laced, and looked up at the night sky. Maybe, he thought, he'd have everything figured out when he woke up the next morning.

21

The next day, just after sunup, Fargo ate his fried bread and thought things over. He was no closer to having them figured out than he'd been when he'd gone to sleep the previous night. In fact, he had more questions now than when he'd lain down.

The thing that kept nagging at him more than any other was the way Slater had responded to his questions just before he'd died. Carter had said that Slater was a liar to the end, but Fargo wasn't so sure. At that point, Slater hadn't had a reason to lie.

What if he'd been telling the truth?

If he had, it would mean that Fargo had been wrong about a lot of things.

For one thing, it would mean that Slater and Logan hadn't started the rumors about Hi Jolly.

It would also mean that Slater and Logan hadn't killed Vinson.

And if they hadn't done those things, who had?

And why?

As Fargo thought, possibilities started to come together in his mind, and he arrived at what might be the answer. But he didn't like it, and he didn't see how it could be right.

He looked around the camp for Clyde Johnson, who was sitting alone with his back resting against a rock, drinking coffee from a battered cup. Fargo walked over and squatted down beside the surveyor.

"Coffee any good this morning?" Fargo asked.

"It has enough dirt and grounds in it to start a coffee farm with," Johnson said. He looked around to see if anyone had heard him. "But it was hot, so don't think I'm complaining."

"Wouldn't expect you to. How's the surveying coming along?"

Johnson poured what remained of his coffee onto the ground. Fargo could see that it was a little thick and grainy, all right.

"We're doing all right," Johnson said, but he was lying and Fargo knew it. Johnson's open, boyish face revealed his thoughts all too clearly.

"That's not what I heard," Fargo said. "I heard that you were having some problems getting things right."

"Who told you that? It must have been Gallagher. He's like an old woman, worrying all the time."

Knowing a little about Gallagher and his past, Fargo could see why he worried. He wasn't necessarily worrying about the survey, though that was no doubt part of it.

"All he does is whine about how we're getting things wrong," Johnson went on. "And how it's causing problems with the mapping."

"If you get things wrong on a map, it can cause a lot of trouble," Fargo said. "For one thing, if people came to Canyon Diablo and thought they had to cross it, they'd be mighty discouraged. They need to know about that river crossing we took, and it has to be in the right place on the map so they won't wander to hell and gone before they find it."

"It'll be in the right place," Johnson said. "I'll see to it that all the coordinates are right."

"What about Montgomery? What will he be seeing to?"

Johnson stood, and so did Fargo.

"Montgomery's doing just fine," Johnson said without conviction.

"You like Jane, don't you?" Fargo said.

Johnson looked at him. "What do you mean by that?"

"Just what I said, that's all."

"I don't much like your tone."

"You're a little touchy this morning," Fargo said. "Is there something you want to tell me, Johnson?"

"If you're implying something about me and Jane,

you're wrong, and I resent it. Now get out of my way and let me go do my job."

Johnson started to move around Fargo, who said, "Your job and Montgomery's, too."

Johnson stopped where he was. His shoulders slumped.

"All right," he said. "Montgomery's not the best surveyor I've ever worked with, but he's doing better all the time. Now leave me alone, Fargo."

"I just have one question for you," the Trailsman said. "Is Montgomery really a surveyor?"

"He's a surveyor. There's not much doubt about that. Or he must have been at one time. He knows enough to get by, but maybe not enough to be as precise as we need to be. But he knows how to use the equipment, even if he's a little rusty. Things are coming back to him. We'll be fine."

"You're not just saying that because you like Jane?"

Johnson looked as angry as Fargo had ever seen him.

"Look, Fargo, you've said about enough."

"I guess I have." Fargo stood aside. "I didn't mean to rile you."

"Well," Johnson said, "you did."

He stalked away, his empty coffee cup dangling from his hand.

Fargo walked to where the camels were being loaded for the day's journey. Hi Jolly was cajoling one of the bigger animals, but it refused to kneel down.

"You worthless spawn of a syphilitic beggar and a crippled mongoose! You pool of yellow ass's drool! You—"

Fargo stopped to listen and admire Hi Jolly's creative cursing. He would have enjoyed hearing more, but Hi Jolly broke off his imprecations when he saw the Trailsman standing there.

"He will cooperate shortly," Hi Jolly said. "The California Camel Corps will not want him if he proves balky."

Fargo mentioned that all the camels were balky.

"True. But they eventually give in, with the proper persuasion. It never fails."

They talked a little more about the camels, and then Fargo asked if Hi Jolly had ever had any run-ins with Robert Montgomery or his daughter.

Hi Jolly shook his head. "Never. They have always been respectful of me and the camels. Not like some of the troopers."

He looked resentfully at the men who were supposed to be helping him, most of whom appeared more interested in avoiding camel bites or kicks than in getting their jobs done.

"Logan and Slater were the worst. They had little liking for me, but I do not know why they did so many bad things."

"Are you sure it was them?"

"And who else would it be? They made it plain that they would like to be rid of me."

"Yeah. But did you ever catch them at any tricks like that scorpion in your blanket? Did you ever hear them saying anything about you?"

"No, I did not. But I know who was behind those things. It was clear to me."

It wasn't clear to Fargo. He'd thought it was, but now he just wasn't sure.

"Well," he said, "you don't have to worry about them anymore."

"No, I do not. But I still have the camels to deal with and all these incompetent do-nothings. I must get back to them."

Fargo agreed and left him to it.

They made good time that morning, and when they stopped at noon Fargo went looking for Randall Gallagher. He wanted to ask about the mapmaking and whether Gallagher thought Montgomery's work was anywhere near accurate.

"Of course it's not," Gallagher said. "I've been telling Clyde that all along, but all he'll say is that it's improving. I think his head's been turned by Montgomery's daughter, if you want to know the truth."

Fargo had already figured that out for himself. He thanked Gallagher for the information and sought out Tolliver. The botanist was sitting in the shade of a wagon. His glasses were pulled down onto the end of his nose, and he was peering over the tops of them at his notebook.

Fargo sat down beside him and said, "I want to ask you something about Vinson."

Tolliver put a dried leaf in his notebook to mark his place. He closed the notebook and stuck it in his pocket.

"I've thought about Vinson a lot," he said. He pushed his glasses back up on his nose. "I wish I could have done more for him."

"What I want to know about is how he might have died," Fargo said. "You said two people might have been able to kill him. Would they have to be strong?"

"Do you mean could Vinson have fought them off?" Tolliver thought it over. "He could have if he'd been awake, maybe not if they caught him while he was sleeping, which is obviously what happened. He did have a broken leg, after all." He paused again. "I'm glad you got those two men, Fargo."

"I'm not so sure they did it," Fargo said. "I thought so at first, but now I'm wondering about it."

"If they didn't do it, who did?"

"I'm not sure yet," Fargo told him, but he was sure only minutes later when Carter came to tell him that the Montgomerys had gone missing.

The way Fargo had it figured, Montgomery and Jane had been behind most of the things Slater and Logan had been blamed for. Or maybe the four of them had been working together.

The accident that had allowed Montgomery to become part of the expedition was just a little too convenient, and the fact that Slater and Logan were newcomers to the army was also suspicious. And of course Montgomery's inability to do his job should have alerted everyone.

Jane, however, had done her part to keep things under control. Fargo didn't know if she'd shared her favors with Johnson, but he wouldn't be surprised to learn that she had. She'd done a good job of lulling Fargo's suspicions with her sexual attentions to him, and at the same time she'd been finding out what he knew, if anything, about her and her father. She could easily have bribed

Johnson with sex to downplay her father's incompetence. Judging from Johnson's behavior that morning, Fargo was inclined to believe that's what had happened.

What Fargo had also decided was that Montgomery and Jane, like Slater and Logan, were after the gold. The fact that there wasn't any gold didn't discourage them, because they refused to believe that. The story of the armor would just have encouraged them further.

And then there was Vinson. He'd told Fargo that there was someone other than Slater and Logan that he was suspicious of. He could have meant the Montgomerys, and if that was the case, they would have had as much reason to kill him as Slater and Logan. Maybe more reason. And Jane had been very attentive to him. If he'd let his suspicions slip, she would have told her father, and that may very well have been the end of Vinson. Jane could have held him down while her father smothered him.

Meanwhile they were using Slater and Logan to start rumors about Hi Jolly so that suspicion would be thrown on him if anything bad happened.

And now they were gone.

Carter explained that they had lingered around at the back of the column for most of the morning, gradually dropping farther and farther behind the others. Nobody had really been paying any attention, and it seemed that they'd eventually just drifted away. Only when the caravan stopped did anyone notice they weren't with the group any longer.

"What're we gonna do about 'em?" Carter asked, although he already had an answer for his own question. "I say we let 'em go. They took some food and water, but they'll never find their way back from out here. From what I hear, Montgomery can't survey his way out of a bedroom, much less find California."

"They might not be headed to California," Fargo said. "They might try to get to the missions down south of here."

"Then I wish 'em luck. Those missions are farther away from us than California is."

"Doesn't matter where they're going," Fargo said. "We have to go after them."

"I don't see why. Better just to let 'em die out here somewhere. Be easier all the way around."

"They might not die, and they should go on trial for what they've done."

"What've they done?"

"They're the ones who killed Vinson."

"Well, goddammit, why didn't you say so. Let's go after the sons of bitches. Dyin's too easy for 'em."

"We need to see Lieutenant Beale first."

"What're we waitin' for?"

"Nothing," Fargo said. "Let's go."

22

They hadn't gone more than half a mile before the Ovaro threw a shoe.

"Maybe that's a sign you should've taken that camel," Carter told Fargo. "Probably the shoe's worn out and the nail heads, too, from this rough ground."

It didn't take Fargo long to discover that Carter was right. The shoe had worn down to the nail heads, which had worn off so that they no longer held the shoe. It had simply slipped off the Ovaro's hoof.

Before they left, Lieutenant Beale had once again insisted that Fargo take Samuel. Fargo didn't mind that Beale wanted to turn in an impressive report to his friends in Washington, but the Trailsman wished that the lieutenant would just leave the camels out of everything that came along.

But at least Beale had understood the need to bring the Montgomerys back.

"If they're responsible for the death of one of my men, I want the army and the courts to deal with them," he said. "Go get them, Fargo."

And that was what Fargo had planned to do. Now it looked as if he was going to be slowed down considerably.

"Good thing we brought a farrier with us," Carter said, as they turned back.

Fargo was riding double with him, and they were leading the Ovaro.

"Gonna take him a while to get the job done, though," Carter said. "You gonna ride the camel? I'd bet the lieutenant's gonna insist on it."

Fargo didn't answer.

*   *   *

Riding the camel wasn't as difficult as Fargo had thought it would be. Hi Jolly pointed out that camels didn't need shoes.

"Which is one of the reasons they're superior to horses for the kind of work they'll be used for on the mail routes," Beale added. "Take the camel, Fargo. You can put it to the test."

Fargo wasn't happy, and neither was Carter. For that matter, neither was the camel, but then Fargo was pretty sure by that time that camels were never happy about anything. However, Beale was the boss, and this time he was insistent.

So Fargo found himself rocking along on top of an animal that smelled like something that had crawled under an outhouse, looking down on Carter and his horse and wishing that he'd never heard of a camel caravan to California.

"You reckon they headed back to those caves?" Carter yelled, looking up at Fargo, who was trying not to sway from side to side with the camel and not succeeding.

"You don't have to yell," Fargo said. "I can hear you."

"Well, you're so high up there, I wasn't sure. What about those caves? You think that's where they're goin'?"

Fargo said he figured that was the Montgomerys' destination, all right. The lure of Coronado's supposed gold and the Spanish armor that had been found in the cave had been more than they could resist.

It was no wonder that both the Montgomerys had been so anxious when Slater and Logan had disappeared. If they'd been working together, then the Montgomerys would have thought that the troopers had betrayed them and were out to get the gold on their own, which Fargo was pretty sure they had been. If they hadn't been working together, then the Montgomerys would have been afraid that Slater and Logan would beat them to the gold and get away with it.

"Reckon they'll find any gold?" Carter said, breaking into Fargo's thoughts. "Or just rattlers."

"There's no gold," Fargo said. "I keep telling everybody that. It's just a legend, an old story that got started

146

some way or other. Once something like that gets going, though, there's no way to stop it."

"That's the God's truth. I bet everybody on this expedition has heard those stories or some like 'em. But not everybody's trying to get the gold."

"Some people have more sense," Fargo said.

"You could be right about that," Carter agreed. "Or maybe they just don't want to run out on their jobs and leave the rest of us to do their part like Montgomery. Kinda crazy to do that. He must have known we'd come after him."

Fargo wasn't so sure. The Montgomerys might have thought the expedition would just let them go. After all, Montgomery wasn't much of a surveyor, and nobody would miss his contributions. But he didn't know that Fargo suspected him and his daughter of killing Vinson.

On the other hand, they might be expecting someone to come after them. In that case, Fargo would make an easy target, riding up so high off the ground. It was a good thing, he thought, that he and Carter were coming up on the caves from the blind side. No one would see them approaching. Unless, of course, one of them was acting as a lookout.

"We'd better act like they know we're coming," Fargo said. "I'd have a long way to fall from this camel if I got shot."

"Well, you'd probably already be dead before you hit the ground if they're any kind of shots," Carter said. "If that's any comfort to you."

"Thanks," Fargo said. "I feel a lot better now."

The camel stopped its usual complaining a mile or so after they left the expedition, but it started up again before they got to the caves.

"They oughta have plenty of warnin' that we're on the way," Carter said. "What you reckon we oughta do about it?"

Fargo didn't know, and he realized as they rode along that there was another difficulty he was going to face. He'd never dismounted from a camel without Hi Jolly's assistance, and he wasn't sure he could do it. Getting on had been difficult enough.

He mentioned the problem to Carter.

"Hell, if you get shot, you'll fall off, so that's taken care of right there."

"You always look on the bright side, don't you," Fargo said.

"I try to. I think that's the best way."

Fargo kept thinking about what he was going to do, and when they came to the fir trees atop the ridge, he solved the problem by guiding the camel under one of its branches. Fargo fought off a face full of fir needles, took hold of the branch, and swung himself off the camel's back.

When he dropped to the ground, Carter said, "That's as graceful a dismount as I ever seen."

Fargo ignored him and tied the camel's halter rope to a lower tree limb.

The camel's only comment on the whole situation was an explosive fart, practically in the face of Carter's mount. The sergeant had to haul back on the reins to keep the horse from bolting.

"If the devil farts," Carter said when he had the horse under control, "that's how it smells. You reckon we've made enough noise up here to warn them good and proper?"

Fargo said he was sure they had. He walked over to the edge of the ridge and looked down, but there was no sign of anyone, and no horses to be seen.

"Maybe they ain't even here," Carter said when he joined him.

"They're here all right," Fargo said.

He'd seen the signs of the two riders along the way, not many but enough to convince him that he and Carter were on the right track.

"Where's the horses?"

"In one of the lower caves," Fargo said. "Or tied off in the trees."

He couldn't see them, but one of those two things had to be the answer.

"Maybe," Carter said. "And what about them two Montgomerys?"

"I'd guess they were in the cave with the armor."

"If they are, they're bein' mighty damn quiet."

"They heard us coming. They'd be quiet."

Carter took off his hat and scratched his head. He

settled the hat back and said, "You reckon they've set a trap for us?"

"I wouldn't be surprised," Fargo told him.

"Any idea what it might be?"

"Not a one. You?"

"Hell, no. So what're we gonna do?"

"Go down there and tell them to surrender."

"You reckon they'll do it?"

"Hell, no," Fargo said.

The trap was better than Fargo had thought it would be. Simple and effective. It worked because Fargo had put too much stock in greed and not enough in cleverness.

Instead of waiting for them in the cave with the armor, Jane and Robert Montgomery had hidden themselves in another cave near the path, and when Fargo and Carter reached the ledge, Robert Montgomery stepped out behind them. He was holding a .45, and he looked as if he was familiar with it.

"We've been expecting you, Fargo," Montgomery said. "I must confess I thought a trailsman would be a bit more careful in his approach."

"It was that damn camel," Carter said.

Montgomery nodded. "Yes. Well, I'm glad to see both of you. Jane and I were getting tired of digging."

Jane stood behind him. She had a pistol, too, but she looked awkward holding it. Fargo suspected that she wasn't a very good shot.

"Take their guns, Jane," Montgomery said. "And please, Fargo, don't try anything. I'll kill both of you, and it won't bother me in the least. I might even hit Jane by accident. You wouldn't want that."

Jane holstered her own pistol and relieved Carter and Fargo of their weapons. Fargo didn't try anything. When she had the pistols, Jane went back behind Montgomery and waited.

"Found any gold?" Fargo said.

"A few snakes is all," Montgomery said. "But we were expecting those. They're dead now. Why don't you and Carter just move along to the cave. You'll find the shovels there already."

"There ain't no gold," Carter said.

His face was red, and Fargo could see that he was mad because they'd fallen for such a simple trap.

"There may not be any gold," Montgomery said. "But we've come a long way to see if there is, so we'll let you dig a while."

"What if we don't find anything?"

"Then there will be a sizeable hole, and you will have saved us the trouble of digging your gaves. Move along now."

Fargo didn't see that they had any choice, so he went on down the ledge to the cave, with Carter right behind him. The Montgomerys followed at a safe distance with their pistols.

When Fargo got to the cave, he saw that there hadn't been much digging. Three snakes lay over on one side, their heads shot off. Montgomery knew how to use the pistol, all right.

The armor and the skeleton had been moved to a spot near the front of the cave, and two shovels leaned against the wall of the cave near a shallow hole.

"You can see that we haven't made much progress," Montgomery said. "I'm a little old for digging, and Jane, while willing, isn't as strong as a man."

"You seem mighty damn spry to me," Carter said. "For an old codger."

"I assure you I'm not as old as I appear. That was just a part of my little deception. I wanted everyone to think I was harmless and a little slow."

"Well, you were a damn poor surveyor, to hear Gallagher tell it."

"I'm out of practice. I did some of that kind of work as a younger man, but I found other pursuits that were more appealing to me."

"Gambling," Fargo said. "That's how you knew Slater and Logan."

"Time to stop talking and get to work," Jane said.

"You're right," Montgomery said. "Pick up a shovel, Fargo, and get started. You too Carter."

It was hot in the cave, and the ground was hard and bone-dry. Fargo and Carter made only slow progress.

While they dug, Montgomery stood well away from

the entrance and talked. It seemed he didn't mind telling them all about himself and Jane, which led Fargo to believe that Montgomery was going to kill them whether they found any gold or not.

From Montgomery's monologue, Fargo learned that he had arranged the accident to the man who'd been hired originally as the expedition's surveyor. Then he'd gotten himself hired because he was looking for the gold he'd heard was buried in the caves.

He'd been a gambler and had known Slater and Logan previously. He recognized them when he got hired as one of Beale's surveyors and knew what they were up to.

"Those two were never cut out to be soldiers," he said.

"You're damn right, they weren't," Carter muttered so that only Fargo could hear him.

They had recognized Montgomery, but so had Vinson, who'd been skinned by him in a card game a few years earlier. Vinson had remembered it after he'd talked to Fargo, and he'd made the mistake of mentioning it to Jane on one of her visits. Just to be on the safe side, Montgomery had eliminated him, with Jane's help. Montgomery knew everyone would suspect Logan and Slater of the murder, if it was ever discovered, a fact which bothered him not in the least.

The three of them, along with Jane, had made a deal to share the gold, but Montgomery doubted Slater and Logan ever considered keeping their part of the bargain. Fargo suspected Montgomery hadn't, either.

"They tried to cheat us," Montgomery said. "I'm glad you took care of them for me, Fargo."

"I didn't do it for you."

"Well, let's say you did it for Jane. Either way, it worked out just fine."

"It's a damn shame that a man would pimp his daughter the way you did," Fargo said.

"Daughter? I told you that I wasn't as old as I looked. I'm older than you, but not by as much as you think. My age was just part of the act, Fargo. Jane's not my daughter. She's my wife."

For the life of him, Fargo couldn't see how that made things any better.

23

After about an hour, Montgomery ran out of talk. Jane hadn't said a word, and Fargo didn't know where she'd gone. Maybe to one of the other caves where she could sit and not have to listen to her husband.

"I'm mighty damn tired of this," Carter said under his breath. "We just gonna dig all day?"

"No," Fargo answered.

"What're we gonna do then? Montgomery's standin' out there with a pistol."

Fargo had been thinking about that. He told Carter to keep digging, to make a lot of noise doing it, and to complain loudly. He had a feeling that was a job Carter could handle, and he was right. The sergeant's shovel scraped the wall and clacked against the stones, and he complained bitterly at the top of his lungs about how hard he was working, how much his back hurt, and how the dust made it hard for him to breathe.

While Carter was doing that, Fargo took the breast-plate and helmet off the skeleton. There were still bits of leathery skin clinging to the bones.

The armor was too small for Fargo, but he could squeeze into the breastplate. He tried to force the helmet on, but he couldn't. He hoped that when Montgomery shot at him, he wouldn't be aiming at his head.

He picked up his shovel. Carter looked at him and stopped talking. Fargo motioned with his hand, and Carter started up again.

When Carter was going strong, Fargo stepped out of the cave. Montgomery saw him and fired before the

Trailsman could reach him, but the bullet zinged off the breastplate.

Fargo didn't give him another chance to shoot. He swung the shovel and knocked the pistol flying. He thought Montgomery would run when he lost the pistol, but he didn't. He lowered his head and ran right at Fargo.

Fargo swung the shovel again, but Montgomery ducked under it, coming in low and wrapping his arms around Fargo's legs. Before Fargo could bring the shovel down on Montgomery's back, the surveyor jerked Fargo's legs out from under him, and Fargo fell backward on the ledge. He hit hard and dropped the shovel. He heard it clatter off the rocks below.

Montgomery jumped quickly to his feet, showing that he was indeed not nearly as old as he'd seemed. He ran back down the ledge, and as Fargo was getting up to go after him, Carter came running out of the cave. Fargo turned to be sure it was Carter, and the sergeant crashed into him. His head hit the breastplate with a loud bong.

Both of them fell. Fargo got up. Carter didn't. He lay on the path with his eyes rolled back in his head.

Fargo didn't have time to see to him. He had to catch Montgomery.

But he was too late. Montgomery had already gotten to the lower level of caves, and by the time Fargo got to the pathway leading down, Montgomery and Jane rode out of the cave on their horses.

Fargo tore off the breastplate and ran up instead of down. He was about to find out how fast a camel could run.

He untied the rope that held the camel and cleared his throat. The camel rumbled a complaint, but it went to its knees. Fargo pulled its head back and got into the saddle. In less time than he would have thought possible, he was on his way.

Samuel was sure-footed, and he carried Fargo down the ridge without faltering in spite of his eccentric gait. As he passed the ledge, Fargo glanced over at Carter, who was sitting up and rubbing his head.

When Samuel reached the bottom of the ridge, Fargo

urged him to go all out, and the camel responded. The rolling ride was enough to make Fargo slightly queasy, but Samuel's speed would have made Hi Jolly proud. It wasn't long before Fargo thought he was actually gaining on Robert and Jane, and soon they were in the river bottom.

Montgomery looked back, saw Fargo gaining on him, and fired a pistol shot in the Trailsman's direction, but he was too far away for any kind of accuracy.

Fargo wondered for a moment where Montgomery had gotten a pistol, but then he remembered. It was the one Jane had taken from him. Fargo pulled out his rifle and tried to adjust for the camel's side to side motion. He fired, missing Montgomery by a good distance.

But he didn't miss Jane, though he hadn't been aiming at her at all. She was riding beside Montgomery, and the motion of the camel had thrown Fargo off just enough. She slumped over her horse's neck, then slid off and hit the ground, hard. The horse ran right on.

Fargo thought Montgomery might stop and help her, but he didn't. He kept on riding. Fargo went after him, gaining all the time.

Before he got too close, he wanted to try another shot with the rifle. This time he got lucky. The bullet plowed into the cantle of Montgomery's saddle. He pitched forward and hit the ground rolling. When he stopped, he came up firing. Fargo heard the lead buzz past his head.

Fargo pulled back on the rope, and Samuel came to a stop. He took his time, aimed the rifle, and shot Montgomery in the shoulder.

Montgomery dropped the pistol and sank to the ground.

All Fargo had to do was go get him.

But he couldn't get Samuel to kneel.

"If I hadn't come along, you'd still be sittin' there on that camel," Carter said as they rode back toward San Francisco Mountain. "I never saw anything like it, and you a grown man."

"I'd like to see you ride a camel," Fargo said.

"I could do it if I wanted to. Don't want to, though.

At least I helped you, which is more'n you did for me. Left me there to die, is what you did."

"I figured your head was hard enough to take a little bump."

Carter put his hand on the bump on his forehead. "Little? Big as a goose egg, if you ask me."

Riding in front of them were the Montgomerys. Robert was slumped in the saddle, barely able to ride. His shoulder was probably shattered and would never heal properly, but he'd live.

Jane was in better shape. Fargo had clipped her arm, taking a little chunk out of the side of it, but that was all. She'd lost some blood by the time Carter had come along to see to her, but she recovered quickly. She still had nothing to say, however.

"What'd you mean about Montgomery panderin' his daughter?" Carter said. "I'd kinda like to hear a little more about that."

"No, you wouldn't," Fargo said.

When the expedition reached Fort Yuma, Lieutenant Beale had the Montgomerys officially arrested, but that was a minor matter. What had him puffed up was the success of the whole affair, discounting a murder and the deaths of a couple of troopers, along with some minor surveying and mapmaking problems.

The camels had done their part, and more. They had shown beyond a doubt that they could hold up under the conditions of the American Southwest, and Beale predicted with confidence that they would play a major part in its development.

"You'll see, Fargo. In ten or twenty years, everyone out here will be riding camels, thanks to the California Camel Corps. We'll establish it right here at Fort Yuma, and it will spread over the country."

Sarah visited Fargo before he left Fort Yuma. She thanked him for everything he'd done.

"I didn't do a thing," he said. "You did it all yourself. I just helped out a little."

"Maybe. But I'm not sure anyone else would have

done what you did for me, and I appreciate it. You'll be leaving now, I guess."

"That's right," Fargo said. "My job's over. I have to find another one."

"Where?"

Fargo waved an arm at the world outside the fort's gates.

"Out there," he said. "Down some trail, over the next hill."

"Do you think you could stay one more night? For me? Just one. I'd like to show my appreciation."

"There are plenty of trails out there," Fargo said. "Plenty of hills. But there's only one of you."

"You can talk pretty when you want to. Does that mean you'll stay?"

"What do you think?"

"I think I'll see you tonight," Sarah said.

Fargo grinned. He was already looking forward to it.

LOOKING FORWARD!
The following is the opening section of the next novel in the exciting *Trailsman* series from Signet:

THE TRAILSMAN #288

GILA RIVER DRY-GULCHERS

The heat could kill. One hundred and fifteen degrees in the shade, and there was precious little shade.

To the big man in buckskins winding through the Gila Mountains it was like being baked alive. But his whipcord body absorbed the blistering heat and did not wither. In him the sun had met its match. He was the man others had taken to calling the Trailsman.

Skye Fargo was taller than most and had shoulders so broad that every woman he met yearned to cling to them. His uncommonly handsome face was framed by a short-trimmed beard and a white hat, now nearly brown with dust. A red bandanna was knotted around his neck. But his most striking feature was his eyes. As blue as a high-country lake, they were the windows to a soul as tough as the land around him. Even tougher, when he had to be. And he might have to be soon.

For the past hour Fargo had been aware of faint sounds behind him. Not faint due to distance but faint because whoever was making the sounds was trying not to let their presence be known. He was being stalked. Since it was extremely unlikely that anyone with friendly intentions would stalk him, he rode with his right hand on the well-worn grips of his Colt and his body half-twisted so that he always had an eye on the winding ribbon of a trail behind him.

Fargo did not know who it was, except that there was more than one. He did know the stalkers were not Apaches. No self-respecting warrior would be so noisy. The Apache moved as silently as a whisper and killed with no forewarning. Whoever was back there had to be white, and not overly bright whites, at that.

Fargo did not stop to wait, nor did he bother to circle around and come up on them from behind. They would make their move when they were ready, and unknown to them, he would be prepared. If he was wrong, if they were not up to no good, all the better. But if there was one lesson he had learned in his years roaming the wilds, it was to regard strangers as enemies until they proved they were friendly.

A bead of sweat trickled from under his hat and left a moist mark down his right cheek. Flicking out his tongue, Fargo licked the drop off before it reached his chin. Such a tiny drop of moisture, yet it was welcome relief to his parched throat. He would be glad when he reached the Gila River, and his destination.

The letter that had brought Fargo to this godforsaken part of the desert Southwest was tucked in his saddlebags. He saw it again in his mind's eye, the neatly penned lines by Clarice Hammond begging him to come help her family find their father. "Implored" was the word Miss Hammond used. Her impeccable grammar suggested to Fargo that she was a lady of breeding and learning. Not exactly the kind of woman he would expect to find in a hellhole like Gila Bend.

The town sprang to life four years ago when a prospector stumbled on a vein of silver. Before you could say lickety-split, hundreds of folks who worshiped at the altar of human greed had turned a strip of land along the Gila River into Gila Bend, yet another boomtown that would go bust the moment the ore ran out. Fargo had seen more than his share of such towns and they were always the same: wild, woolly, and deadly for those who were not quick with a gun or quicker with their wits.

Fargo was not one to brag, but he was both. Otherwise he would not have survived as long as he had. He never sought trouble, but neither did he run from it when it came his way—as those behind him were about to learn.

In another half an hour Fargo came to where the trail widened near the base of a giant stone slab. Reining up in the slab's shadow, he stiffly dismounted, then stretched. His pinto was layered with sweat and wearily hung its head. "We don't have far to go, boy," he assured it. "Tonight you'll rest in a stable and eat your fill of oats."

The mention of food, even if for his horse, made Fargo's stomach rumble. He had been living on pieces of pemmican and jerky for the past week, and he was looking forward to a thick, juicy steak with all the trimmings.

Then hooves clattered, and Fargo put all thoughts of steak from his mind and turned to confront the three men who were riding toward him with smiles plastered on their grime-streaked faces. He pretended to be just as sociable and smiled back. "Howdy, gents." But his thumb was hooked in his gun belt close to his Colt, and his rifle was within easy reach in his saddle scabbard.

The trio were cut from the same coarse cloth. Their clothes were as dirty as they were, their boots badly scuffed. Two sported unkempt beards. The third, the rider in the lead, was a small man with ferret features and ferret eyes and stubble dotting his ferret chin. He was the dangerous one, the one whose eyes gleamed with craftiness. The one most likely to shoot Fargo in the back if Fargo was fool enough to turn it to him.

"Howdy, there, friend," the ferret declared. "You must be bound for Gila Bend, the same as us."

"Must be," Fargo said. Inwardly he smiled when all three glanced at his right hand, and the Colt.

The ferret and his companions reined up and the ferret took off his short-brimmed hat and wiped his brow with a dusty sleeve. "Folks hereabouts call me Spack. These are my pards, Grub and Toad."

Fargo went on smiling but did not tell them his name as they were waiting for him to do.

"Well," Spack said amiably. He replaced his hat and tugged on the brim. "I reckon I can't blame you for not tellin' us who you are, what with all the killin's and such the past month and a half."

"Been a lot, has there?" Fargo asked.

"Mister, you wouldn't believe it," Spack said. "Nineteen people have gone missin' and eleven others have been found murdered. It's gettin' so a decent hombre can't go anywhere unless he's got eyes in the back of his head."

"I know the feeling," Fargo responded dryly.

Spack gazed at the surrounding range. The Gila Mountains were low and barren, the highest peak not much over three thousand feet high. Compared to the Rockies they were more like hills, but they were as stark and rugged as their much higher kin, and certain death to the unwary. "This is a hard land."

"Hard enough," Fargo agreed. The other two were slowly moving their mounts to either side while trying not to be obvious about it. Amateurs, he thought with scorn, and they would get what they had coming.

Spack went on talking, trying to lull him into making a mistake. "They say most of the people who went missin' were taken by the Renegade."

"Who?"

"That's what they call him. The Renegade. No one has ever laid eyes on him but they reckon he's an Apache. Who else would carve 'em up so?"

"You've lost me," Fargo admitted.

"The bodies that have been found," Spack said. "Most of 'em were cut up somethin' awful. Noses gone, ears chopped off, tongues cut out, that sort of thing." He scowled. "Everyone knows how Apaches like to whittle on whites."

"But why do they think it's just one?" With the tally at thirty, Fargo was inclined to think a war party was to blame.

" 'Cause tracks have been found near some of the bodies," Spack related. "Moccasin prints. Apache moccasins. And only one set."

"Which Apache tribe?" Fargo inquired. No two tribes made their moccasins exactly alike. An experienced tracker could always tell the difference. "Chiricahuas? Or the Mimbres?"

"How would I know? And who the hell cares? Redskins are redskins. We'd all be better off if every last one of the stinkin' heathens was six feet under."

"That's right," the one called Grub said. "It was Apaches killed my brother. Tied him upside down to a fence post, they did, and baked his brains."

"They don't like having their territory invaded," Fargo remarked.

"Invaded?" Spack snorted. "Whose side are you on, anyhow? So what if they were here before us? We're here now, and it's us or them who has to go away and it sure as hell won't be us."

"I hear that," Grub said gruffly.

Toad had not said a word. He was too busy cleaning out his left ear with his little finger. He wiped the wax off on his pants, then commented, "These parts aren't safe, no sir. It'd be smart if you rode with us."

Spack shot him a nasty look, as if Spack had wanted to make the offer himself, then smiled his oily smile. "Toad has a point. If you don't mind the company, you're welcome to tag along with us for protection."

"That's decent of you," Fargo said, trying not to laugh. "But I can manage on my own."

"Are you sure, friend?" Spack asked. "Extra guns in Apache country can come in mighty handy."

Fargo had no intention of riding with them just so they could fill him with lead at the first opportunity. Then again, it wouldn't do to have them go on stalking him, either. It made more sense to stick close so he could keep an eye on them. "You've changed my mind. I'll tag along after all."

"Smart man," Spack said by way of false pride. "You won't regret it. We're bound to make it to town in one piece." When Fargo just stood there he asked, "What are you waitin' on?"

"My horse needs some rest," Fargo explained. "Go on ahead if you want. I'll catch up."

Spack did not like it but he forced a grin and a nod. "Whatever you want, mister. We'll be takin' our sweet time so there's no need to rush." Touching his hat brim, he clucked to his buttermilk.

Fargo watched the trio wind on down the mountain until they were out of sight. Mounting, he left the trail, picking his way with care through boulders and scrub brush until he was fifty yards out. Then he reined to the southwest. Soon he had caught up to the cutthroats and was paralleling them with them none the wiser.

They thought they had pulled the wool over his eyes. Joking and laughing, they never once gazed in Fargo's direction. Half a mile further on the trail narrowed, passing between two boulders the size of buffalo. Spack reined up. The three climbed down, and Spack had Grub stand behind one boulder and Toad behind the other with their rifles in hand.

Fargo reached for his Henry but let go of it without sliding it out. He squinted up at the burning sun, then at the three hardcases who were waiting for him to come along the trail so they could dry-gulch him, and he grinned. It would be an hour or more before they grew impatient and one of them rode back to see what had happened to him. An hour or more of the sweltering inferno. Chuckling, Fargo rode on, and when he was gone far enough to be safe, he returned to the trail and continued on his way.

Heat rose off the ground in unrelenting waves. The air itself was hot, and breathing it was like breathing fire. Fargo would just as soon be up in the Tetons at that time of year, but he could use the three hundred dollars Clarice Hammond was offering for his services. He had lost nearly every cent he had in a poker game a few weeks before.

Fargo thought again of her letter, and her missing father. He wondered if her father had fallen prey to the

Renegade. If so, tracking down a lone Apache would take some doing. It posed more of a challenge than looking for the proverbial needle in a haystack, particularly since the needle would be out to kill.

The afternoon waxed and waned. The sun was nearing the western horizon when Fargo rounded a bend, and there, not far below, was a welcome sight.

Gila Bend, situated on the north side of the Gila River at a point where the river started to flow to the northwest along the edge of the Gila Mountains, was a motley collection of frame buildings and false fronts sprinkled with cabins and tents. Very few people were braving the heat but that would change once the sun went down.

His pinto quickened its pace without being prodded. The trail came out on flatland a quarter of a mile southeast of town. Fargo reined toward the river. At that time of year it was more akin to a creek but his throat didn't care. Water was water, and he lay on his belly and drank in great gulps, the pinto at his side. Smacking his lips, Fargo sat up and removed his hat and his bandanna. He dipped the bandanna in the river, wrung it out, and wiped the dust from his face and neck. A wonderful feeling of coolness spread over him but it was short-lived. Soon he was back in the saddle.

The sun was half gone when Fargo reached Gila Bend. Long shadows cast the buildings in preternatural twilight. As he predicted, more people were moving about, a surprising number of them women. Or maybe not so surprising. Where there were riches to be made there were fallen doves out to separate the men who earned the riches from their money.

The grandest of the buildings was the Gila Hotel. By St. Louis or Kansas City standards it was second-rate, but it was the only building in town three stories high, and one of the few with glass in the windows. Four of five rocking chairs on a newly built boardwalk were occupied by ladies in bright dresses who brazenly regarded Fargo as a butcher might a fresh haunch of meat.

The fifth chair was filled by a gray-haired gentleman in a suit who arched a graying eyebrow and said, "What have we here? Another sheep to the slaughter. Another lamb to be fleeced."

"How's that?" Fargo asked, adjusting the saddlebags he had thrown over his left shoulder. In his right hand was the Henry.

"Hold on to your poke or you won't have it long," the oldster warned. "If it's not a long-legged female who will get her hooks into you, it will be a cardsharp or a pickpocket."

"I don't fleece easy," Fargo said, "and I take it you have your poke."

The old man laughed. "Tricking someone my age takes some doing. But I take back what I said. It's plain as the wart on my nose that you're no greenhorn." He offered a bony hand. "Fenton Wilson, at your service. I own this hotel."

"You?" Fargo could not keep the mild surprise out of his voice.

"What? I have too many gray hairs? Or should I be off in the mountains, risking life and limb for a paltry handful of rocks?" Fenton shook his head. "That's not for me, thank you very much. There are smart ways to make a living and there are dumb ways to make a living and if I haven't learned the difference at my age, take me and put me out of my misery."

Fargo shook. Wilson's skin reminded him of old leather but there was genuine warmth in the man's shake and in his expression. "I need a room."

"Would that I had one," Fenton said. "Mine have all been full every night ever since I had the place built."

"I was told there's one reserved in my name," Fargo said, and told the old-timer who he was.

Wilson blinked, then said, "Well now." Slowly rising, he gestured for Fargo to go in ahead of him. "As a matter of fact, there is. Been holding it for weeks now." He looked Fargo up and down. "So you're him? The one they write about? Daniel Boone and Kit Carson rolled into one?"

"I'm just me," Fargo said. At moments like this he wished he could get his hands on the hacks who churned out story after story about every frontiersman of note, tales as tall as any ever told by a mountain man. The West was exciting news to the millions back East who lived drab lives but hankered after adventure, and the monthlies and the newspapers did their best to feed the demand.

The lobby was a haven for those not yet ready to brave the lingering heat of the fading day. Some sat, more stood, all chatting or reading or otherwise whiling away their time until the sun went down.

Fenton Wilson led Fargo to a counter near a flight of stairs and pushed a register toward him. "An X will do if you can't write."

Fargo signed his full name and was given the key to room 303. "It's on the third floor, toward the back. The Hammonds have six rooms, counting yours."

"Why so many?" Fargo wondered. Clarice Hammond had mentioned her family in the letter but had not said how many were with her.

"They wanted a suite and it's the best I could do," Fenton said. "One room for the mother, Janet, one room for each of the two daughters, Clarice and Millicent, a room for each of the bothers, Frank and Dexter, and a room for you."

"Are they up there now?" The sooner Fargo looked them up, the sooner he got his hands on the three hundred dollars.

"I don't believe so, no," Fenton replied. "They went out about half an hour ago. Down to Maxine's, if I recollect correctly, for supper. They eat early, those Hammonds. Comes from being from New Jersey, I suppose."

Fargo leaned his elbows on the counter. "What can you tell me about the father? They've hired me to try and find him."

"I know," Fenton said. Bending forward, he lowered his voice. "If you ask me, son, you've come all this way for nothing. As sure as I'm standing here, that jackass went and got himself killed. The only thing left to find of Desmond Hammond are his bones, and that's only if the scavengers have left any."

"How long has he been missing?"

"Let's see now. It'll be two months come the end of this week. He went off into the mountains on one of his many trips to find silver and never came back."

Fargo let out a sigh. He agreed with Fenton. After two months there was no hope in hell the father was still alive. It was too bad Clarice failed to mention it in her letter. Fenton was right about something else: he had come all this way for nothing. "Where do I find Maxine's?"

"Take a right out the door and go two blocks," Wilson said. "You can't miss it. Your nose will think it's in heaven." He paused. "But if you want to clean up first, I've got a tub in the back. I charge most folks a dollar for a bath but you can have one for free."

"Why so generous?" Fargo wanted to know.

Fenton Wilson shrugged. "I don't know. I reckon I've taken a shine to you, and I don't take a shine to many." He acted embarrassed by the admission. "So what do you say?" he gruffly demanded. "Do you want the bath or not?"

Fargo was hungry enough to eat a buffalo, but he was more than a little whiffy from the long ride. It would not do to meet Clarice Hammond smelling like the south end of a northward horse. "I'm obliged."

"Don't make a mountain out of an anthill of kindness."

Fargo placed the Henry and his saddlebags on the counter. "Can you have these taken up to my room?"

"Consider it done." Fenton picked up a bell and rang it. Within seconds a cherubic youngster materialized at Fargo's elbow.

"Yes, sir, Mr. Wilson, sir."

"Donny, this gentleman is to be treated to a bath on the house, and I—" Fenton abruptly stopped. "What's the matter with you, boy? Why is your mouth hanging open like that?"

"Did you say he gets his bath for free?" Donny was incredulous.

"Another smart-aleck remark like that and you'll be

sweeping horse droppings for a living," Fenton warned. "Yes, I said for free, and what of it? You're to tend to the water personally and supply him with a towel and a bar of lye soap. Understood?"

"Yes, sir," Donny responded, but he still sounded as if he could not credit his ears. To Fargo he said, "This way, sir, if you please." He hustled past the counter and down a narrow hall to a door at the back. Working the latch, he stepped aside. "After you, sir."

Fargo entered. In addition to the tub there was a bench for his clothes and a small open window high in the rear wall. He turned, and found the youngster studying him as if he were a form of life the boy had never set eyes on before. "What?"

"Are you God Almighty, sir?"

"Are you drunk, boy?" Fargo rejoined.

"Oh, no, sir," Donny took him seriously. "My ma would take a switch to me if I so much as sniffed a glass of beer."

"I've been asked some dumb questions but that takes the prize. Next you'll want to know if silver grows on trees."

Donny smiled self-consciously. "I didn't mean it like that, sir. It's just that Mr. Wilson never does anything for free. *Never*," he stressed. "You must be awful special for him to treat you like this."

"I scout and track for a living," Fargo said. "Nothing special there." He also spent a lot of time at card tables and had been known to tip a bottle or three when he had time on his hands.

"Maybe so," Donny said. "But it's mighty strange Mr. Wilson is being so kind. He still has the first dollar he ever made. He told me so."

Fargo took off his hat and hung it on a peg. "There's always more to people than we think there is."

"Maybe so," Donny repeated, "but if I didn't know I was awake, I'd think I was dreaming."

It took seven trips for the boy to fill the tub, toting two full buckets of piping hot water from the kitchen each trip. The room became steamy.

Fargo waited for the last bucket to be poured, then slid a small roll of bills from his pocket and peeled off a five. "My horse is the pinto out front at the hitch rail. Take him to the livery and put him up for the night. I saw a sign that says it's two dollars so you give the liveryman the five and keep the three for yourself."

Donny's lower jaw had a habit of dropping like a trapdoor. "All *three,* sir? I can bring you the change if you want."

"All three," Fargo said. He had been the boy's age once, and hardly ever had fifty cents to his name. "But you have to go back to the livery later and make sure the liveryman has my pinto tucked away nice and cozy. Do we have a deal?"

"Mister, for three dollars I'd go after the Renegade with my slingshot," Donny declared, holding the bill as if it were the Holy Grail. "Anything you want, you just give a holler."

"I could use a towel and that bar of soap," Fargo reminded him, and the boy lit out of there like his britches were on fire. Donny was back in three shakes of a mule's tail and then whisked out again to tend to the pinto.

Fargo unbuckled his gun belt and placed it on the bench at arm's length from the tub. He stripped off his boots, shirt and pants, placing them beside it. He was about to shed his socks when he heard the door open. "Donny, that you?" he asked, glancing over his shoulder.

"Not hardly," Spack said as he, Grub and Toad sauntered in. "Remember us? We've been lookin' for you, you coyote."